Delilah

L.L. MECAZANI

EVELLI

Publisher's Cataloging-In-Publication Data

Mecazani, L. L.
  Delilah / L.L. Mecazani.

    pages ; cm. -- ([Bethany Jasdam series] ; [1])

    Issued also as an ebook.
    ISBN: 978-0-578-16251-5

    1. Older people--Home care--Fiction. 2. Older people--Crimes against--Fiction. 3. Murder--Fiction. 4. Mystery fiction. I. Title.

PS3613.E339 D45 2015
813/.6   2015941069

Cover design: Encircle Publication
Interior design: Christine Keleny ⁴ CKBooks Publishing

To the memory of the three people who inspired me to write this story.

꙳

To my children and grandchildren who are the wind beneath my wings.

꙳

To my husband, who makes my life worth living. His love and support have gotten me through the past forty-two years and made this book possible.

As the lines of the Celtic knot are interwoven, so too is each life interwoven in each other life it encounters. Choices each person makes ultimately affect many others through eternity. Though each loop in the knot, and each life, is individual, one cannot be separated from the other, whether the loops of the knot or the whole of mankind.

L.L. Mecazani

Chapter 1

Bethany Jasdam longed to forget what her mother had done. She was sitting, curled up on her loveseat, watching some birds eating out of feeders in her backyard. For that moment, as she finished her morning coffee, she felt relaxed and peaceful. That feeling was soon to fade as she thought about the day that lay ahead. Beth sighed, put down her cup, and finished getting ready for their trip.

Beth and her husband were heading to Johnston, Wisconsin, a three hour drive from their hometown of Green Bay. Johnston was where her father was born and raised, and now had become his final resting place. The local Johnston hospice held a memorial service each year for loved ones who had died, whether or not hospice was involved in their care. Beth had been invited every year for the past three years because of her father, Mike, but every year she had declined. This year she agreed to go but wondered if she had made a mistake. As in the past years, she dreaded the possibility of her mother, Delilah, also attending. Beth shuddered at the thought.

Beth stood watching her husband, Edward, back their car out of the garage. In the sunlight, the newly fallen snow looked like diamonds scattered in the driveway. As she walked to the car, into the brisk air, she pulled up the hood of her coat, glad to have dressed for the weather.

It was a quiet journey, Beth so deep in thought; she didn't even hear Edward ask how she was doing. She watched out the car window, surrounded by the majesty of the season.

"Isn't it beautiful?" Beth said.

"It sure is," Edward replied.

"I think my Dad would be happy we are attending the service."

"I'm sure he would be, but he was happy with you no matter what you did. You made your Dad a happy man, just like you make me happy."

Beth reached over and squeezed Edward's hand. "Thanks."

The plows had been out so at least the roads were clear, making the three hours pass by quickly. As they approached their destination, they saw the town aglow with Christmas lights and heard Christmas carols playing through loudspeakers placed strategically around town.

Beth smiled to herself as she saw a billboard that read *Remember the reason for the season.* She agreed; Christmas had become way too commercial.

Beth and Edward made their way to the old church building, which had been converted into a community center, where they were greeted by a smiling hospice worker. They were given a program that included the names of all who would be remembered that day. Beth glanced at the names until she found her father listed. She could not help being overcome with grief. Edward put his strong arm around her shoulders while gently pulling her close to his tall, muscular body. Beth rested her head against his chest.

His soft, brown doe-eyes gazed down at her as he bent down and kissed her forehead. "You know your father would not want you to be sad."

Beth nodded and dried the tears that by now were streaming down her face. When her father died, he left a hole in her heart so large she believed it would never be filled. Beth missed him greatly.

"I'm so grateful I was with my dad when he died and had the opportunity to say goodbye. Thank you for allowing me to spend that time with him."

Edward took her hand and squeezed. Beth was thankful for the comfort and love Edward so easily gave her.

They stepped into the community room, and Beth felt her heart begin to pound as her hands turned clammy and her knees lost their ability to hold her upright. She grasped Edward's arm for support as her heart sank to her stomach. Edward squeezed her hand a little tighter. He felt her whole body trembling as he guided her to one of the chairs lined up for the service.

"What's wrong?" he asked. "You seem like you're afraid of something."

"My worst fear has just been realized."

"What's that?"

"I just noticed my mother is here."

"Really, where? I didn't see her."

"Just behind us," Beth whispered, inclining her head to the left.

Edward turned around and saw his mother-in-law sitting next to a white-haired, older man just left of the entry. Delilah was easily recognizable by her short, pure white hair, which made her stand out in the crowd. She had the body of a young boy, yet when she walked, she swaggered like she thought she was a bombshell. Wrinkles riddled every inch of her light complexion, and when she smiled, yellow teeth protruded from her gums. The couple had a group of people around them.

"She always has to be the center of everything," Beth said.

Sitting where she could see everyone that came into the room gave Delilah the opportunity to talk to people she wanted information from, giving her more to gossip about. It also brought searing looks to those Delilah did not like, which after years of listening to Delilah complain, Beth decided, was almost everyone. Despite this fact, Delilah managed to charm many people into believing they were her friends. This assured Delilah that she would always be surrounded by a crowd, her favorite place to be.

"I think that man sitting next to her is with her."

"Who is he?"

"I don't know. I've never seen him before, but from the description my Aunt Louise gave me, I think it is her slattern, Leo."

Beth had been told by her Aunt Louise that Leo and Delilah had been "rolling around in the slop like a bunch of pigs" for over two years. Beth's father, Mike, had only been dead three years. Beth's heart ached for her father. She couldn't believe that Delilah, even with her cold heart, could have gotten over him so quickly.

The service was beautiful, and as they read her father's name, Beth wiped away a stream of warm tears that were falling to her cheeks. Beth, once again, was thankful to have Edward beside her. Edward had always been Beth's rock and continued to support and comfort her through all that she had endured. Beth believed theirs was a marriage made in heaven and thanked God every day for bringing him into her life. Growing up, Delilah had made Beth's life miserable, so Beth believed Edward saved her, and she was extremely grateful to him. That made her love for him even stronger.

Refreshments were available after the service, and while Beth was eating a delicious, freshly-baked, Christmas sugar cookie, she overheard Delilah, who positioned herself within earshot of Beth, talking to someone.

"Beth has no business being here since she has decided not to be part of my life." Delilah then turned and glared at Beth, and the evil that Beth knew so well behind the charming façade seared right through her.

Beth turned to her husband. "We need to leave now."

Edward looked over Beth's shoulder at Delilah's menacing stare. He grabbed Beth's hand and they headed out the door.

"I'm sorry your mother ruined what should have been a beautiful day for you. I know how anxious you were to honor your father today." He gently kissed her cheek.

Beth and Edward drove to the cemetery on the other side of town where Mike was buried. Beth longed to spend time with her father, and Edward was happy to oblige. The snow had made the roads into the cemetery impassable by car, so Beth and Edward trudged through knee-deep snow to make their way to her father's grave. Beth stood in the cold and snow, missing her father more than ever. Uncontrollable tears streamed down Beth's cheeks, the cold wind almost causing the tears to turn to ice. Edward put his arm around Beth and held her close as she stood shivering.

As they turned to walk back to the car, Beth gazed at the graves of her other loved ones. She turned to Edward.

"What would you think if next year I included all of my family members here in the memorial service? I feel that would be my way of honoring them."

"I think that would be a great idea. That would show how much you loved them and miss them."

Snow had begun to gently fall as Beth and Edward got into their car. The day left Beth emotionally exhausted. She was eager for the warm welcome her home would provide. She was glad they had moved to Green Bay from Chicago several years before. Green Bay was only a three hour journey from Johnston, while Chicago was eight, and today that meant she would feel the security of home sooner.

"I see sadness in your eyes," Edward said before he started the car. "What is bothering you, sweetheart? Was it seeing your mother, or are you sad because you miss your father?"

"Yes, I do miss my father, and yes I'm upset with my mother. But I'm sad because I am the only one who truly understands the person my mother is, and because of the pain my mother continues to inflict on me. Being an only child, it's difficult for me; it means that I have to carry the burden of my mother myself. I have always wished for a sibling, while at the same time, I'm thankful that I was the only child to feel my mother's anger. I am also thinking about Leo, wondering if he is someone, in the long line of people, my mother has manipulated into believing she cares about."

As they pulled out of the parking lot, Beth started planning how she would include all of her relatives in the memorial service next year and her mind wandered back to the odd events that took those lives.

Chapter 2

Beth's thoughts began with her grandmother, Helen Marin, and her husband, Sam. Sam was born in Michigan after his parents and oldest brother emigrated from Europe. Sam moved to Johnston with his parents and nine siblings in 1914. Sam and Helen met when Helen emigrated from Europe and settled in Johnston with her parents, her brother, John, and her sister, Katherine. They were both young teenagers when they met, and over the course of several years, they courted and fell in love.

They were both nineteen when they married, not uncommon for the time. Together they produced four sons. Their first son, Sam Jr., died in infancy. Their second son was Beth's father, Mike. The other two were Beth's uncles, Paul and Joey. Paul had died in his early thirties, so only Mike and Joey remained.

Sam and Helen were married almost fifty years until Sam's death in 1975.

Helen was a delicate, fragile woman. She stood only four feet nine inches tall and weighed about ninety pounds. She had light brown eyes and, surprisingly, despite her advanced age, coal black hair, which she kept cut short in a very tight permanent. Helen called it her "poodle cut." This was the only style Beth ever remembered Helen having. Because she was of small stature, she had been protected by everyone in her life, including her parents, siblings, Sam and their children, and eventually Beth.

After Sam died, Helen began to show signs of early dementia. In thinking about it, Beth remembered that she had been showing signs for about a year before that. Everyone in the family felt that Sam had protected Helen and did not allow the signs of dementia to show. Beth recalled him interrupting her speech or making excuses for her behavior.

With Sam gone, Delilah began making all the decisions concerning Helen. Just a week after Sam died, Beth got a call from her Uncle Joey's wife, Louise.

"I'm worried about your grandma, Beth. The other day, I stopped by to see how she was getting along and I discovered that she had left the flame burning on her kitchen stove."

"That doesn't sound good," Beth said.

"That's when I called your mom and asked her to come over to Helen's. Your mother decided Helen could not live alone anymore, and without consulting anyone, she decided to take Helen home to live with her and Mike.

"I told her I didn't think that was necessary. Since we live in the same building as Helen, I could keep an eye on her. That way she could stay in the apartment she has lived in for over twenty-five years. That would be less traumatic for her, especially since she's still adjusting to life without Sam," Louise said.

"But you know your mother. She told me, 'I don't care what you think; I'm taking her home with me. If Joey has anything to say about it, he can talk to Mike.' She tried to justify it by saying that Mike is older and it should be his decision where Helen lives."

Both Beth and Louise knew that in the past, Delilah had tried to manipulate Helen but Sam had always blocked her plans. Beth remembered a time when Delilah decided she would take Helen to Doctor Cube for a checkup. Sam found out and refused to allow it. He took the day off work and took Helen to her own doctor. When it was decided that Helen needed surgery, Delilah wanted Helen to go to the hospital Delilah always used. Sam arranged for Helen to have surgery at the hospital her doctor recommended, and did not tell Delilah the date of Helen's surgery. He accompanied his wife and stayed with her the whole day. When he returned home that night, he phoned

Mike, informing him of Helen's surgery. When Mike relayed the information to Delilah, she began to scream at him, telling him what an asshole his father was. She slapped Mike when he tried to stand up for his parents and threatened to divorce him, saying that he liked his parents more than her. Now that Sam was gone, Delilah was free to do as she wished. They also knew that no one could stop her because Delilah would fly off into a rage at anyone who tried.

Beth didn't know what to say. She wanted to help Helen but she felt unable to. Beth remembered the beatings she suffered as a child at Delilah's hand, simply because she did not respond quickly enough or give the answer Delilah wanted. So even though Beth no longer lived with Delilah, she still felt paralyzed by her.

Louise had heard about these incidents from her husband, so she didn't want to anger Delilah and suffer the same abuse or, heaven forbid, have Delilah take her anger out on Helen.

"I told her that I wasn't sure Joey would agree with moving his mother and that I had helped Sam care for Helen for several years. I know this is where Sam would want her to stay, and I told her so."

"What did she say to that?" Beth asked, surprised by Louise's determination to stand up to Delilah.

"She said if anyone would have told her that Helen had dementia, she would have helped, though I find that highly unlikely. I don't mean to be rude, Beth, but whenever there is work to do, your mother always seems to have other plans."

Beth nodded her head in agreement even though Louise couldn't see her over the phone lines.

"Then she told me she didn't care what Joey or I thought and that she and Mike are going to pick her up tomorrow afternoon. I tried to convince her that Joey wouldn't like having Helen moved, but she wouldn't hear it."

"Then what happened?"

"She just told me that I should have Helen ready."

Chapter 3

Louise asked Beth to be with her the next afternoon since Joey would be at work. Joey had called and asked to talk to Mike but Delilah wouldn't give him the phone. He tried to talk Delilah out of moving Helen, but he didn't have any more luck than Louise had. Delilah was going to pick Helen up regardless of Joey's protests.

When Delilah arrived, Louise decided she would try to reason with her one last time.

She swallowed hard. "Joey is not happy about this. He believes moving Helen will only add to her confusion."

"I don't give a shit whether or not Joey is happy. She's coming with me."

Delilah walked past Louise, bumping into her and knocking her into the cook stove. Beth and Louise stood shaking their heads in disbelief.

14

Delilah crossed the kitchen and entered the living room. One of the doors off the living room was Helen's bedroom. Delilah began forcefully opening dresser drawers, throwing Helen's clothes into a shopping bag. She walked back into the kitchen where Helen was seated at the table and grabbed more grocery bags and walked back to Helen's room.

Helen was looking down at the floral design on her tabletop. She lifted her eyes to look at Louise. "I'm frightened."

"You'll be okay, Helen," Louise responded, while beads of perspiration crossed her forehead. She looked at Beth. "I sure hope you'll be okay." Beth walked over to Helen and held her hand, which was shaking uncontrollably.

Delilah finished her packing, walked back into the kitchen, and grabbed Helen's wrist. "Come on, let's go."

Helen began to cry. "Where are you taking me? I want to stay home."

"You can't stay home alone," Delilah said, her voice cracking with anger.

Delilah opened the apartment door, pulling Helen by her wrist.

Tears were streaming down Helen's face. "I don't want to go!"

Beth and Louise both called to Helen, "Goodbye Grandma, we'll see you soon."

Beth was shaking, recalling the abuse she suffered

at Delilah's hand, afraid the same would happen to Helen, yet feeling helpless not knowing what to do to stop it. She sat down in the kitchen chair, remembering happier times there.

Since Helen's son, Joey, and Beth were close in age, Helen treated Beth in the same manner she treated Joey. Beth and Joey would walk to Joey's home from school together where they were greeted by Helen, who had just poured them each an ice-cold glass of milk and set out a plate of warm, freshly-baked cookies. Helen usually made chocolate chip since she knew they were Beth's favorite. Sometimes they would walk home for lunch together, too. Helen would make their lunch and allow them to sit in the living room and watch *Garfield Goose* before heading back to school. Beth enjoyed her time with Joey and her grandmother. She was never treated that lovingly by her mother. Delilah did not have time for Beth, which is why she spent so much time with Helen.

Helen taught Beth to cook, clean the house, and even how to clean fish. She would sit with Beth for hours reminiscing about her life in Europe before she immigrated to the United States.

"I loved to go to my Aunt Helen's house in the old country," her grandmother told her. "She was always a lot of fun. We would run through the fields and pick flowers for her great big kitchen table. Her house always smelled so good. Something was always cooking or in the oven.

I would help her roll out cookie dough and form shapes with different cutters. She sat and read to me and told me stories of my grandparents and fun times she had with my mother when they were growing up. She told me I held a special place in her heart since I was named after her. I sure do miss her."

"It sounds like you had fun in the old country," Beth said.

"Yes, I did. I wish I could see everyone again. I will never be able to go back to the old country, and besides, most of them are dead anyway." Helen wiped a tear from her eye.

"That must make you sad, but at least you can remember them."

"Yes, I'm glad I have my memories. I also still have my mother, my sister, Katherine, and my brother, John. Sometimes we all sit and remember together. When we are all together, I miss my dad too."

"You're lucky. I don't have a brother or sister. Sometimes it gets lonely," Beth answered with sadness in her voice. "But I'm glad I have my dad."

"I'm glad I have a brother and sister. I'm also glad I had nice grandparents and Aunt Helen. They always told me I was special and protected me. They made me feel safe."

"I'll protect you too, Grandma. I love you," Beth said as she gently patted her grandmother's arm. "Let's eat cookies!"

א

Helen had learned to be trusting of everyone, and now that dementia had set in, she became even more trusting. After years of observing Delilah's behavior with Helen before Sam's death, Beth knew all Delilah wanted was to control Helen.

After Helen had moved in with Beth's father and mother, Beth recalled one Sunday afternoon while Mike, Delilah, and Helen were visiting Beth at her home, Mike took Beth aside, hoping Delilah would not see.

"You will not believe what your mother is up to. She took Grandma to our attorney to draw up a will. She said she made sure that I would be executor but she wouldn't tell me anything else about it. Then she took Grandma to all of the banks in which Grandma has accounts and put my name on all of the accounts. She had my name included on the title of the apartment building Dad and Mom lived in and owned for almost twenty-five years. And she did all of this without anyone's knowledge. When she gave me the paperwork to sign, I asked why Joey's name had not been included on anything. She said to just sign without question or she would divorce me and I would be left without anyone to care for Grandma. I didn't feel I had a choice, so I signed."

"I'm sure that was hard for you to do, Dad, but I agree, I don't think you had a choice. I know if you didn't do what Mom demanded, she would have made your life miserable. I'm so sorry. I wish I could help, but I don't think there's anything I can do. Mom doesn't listen to me. She doesn't listen to anybody."

"I know, Beth. I just feel so bad. What am I going to tell Joey?"

"He will understand. Everyone knows how manipulative Mom is. I'm also sure Joey believes you will do what's best."

א

Shortly after the documents were signed and everything was finalized, Delilah convinced Mike to sell Helen's apartment building. Since Joey and Louise lived in one of the apartments, they would soon find themselves without a place to live. Luckily, they had been able to save up a down payment for a home where they could live with their three children.

After they moved into their house, Delilah called Louise.

"I've decided I don't want this witch here all of the time. You will take her every other week."

"I'd be glad to keep Helen full time. You don't have to keep her at all."

"I'll decide if and when I'll keep the witch. You will keep her when I say you will keep her. I'll bring her over tomorrow afternoon, if I don't kill her before that."

Louise shook her head in dismay. She knew Delilah was all talk but she still didn't like the way she spoke. "I won't be home tomorrow afternoon. The kids have a program at school."

"I don't care. Figure it out. I'll be there at two."

"I won't be here," Louise insisted.

"Then I'll leave her on your front steps," Delilah snarled. "If something happens to her, it will be your fault."

"Maybe Joey can take tomorrow afternoon off of work."

"I don't care who is there. The witch will be dropped off at two."

When Mike returned home from work, Delilah told him of her plan.

"Your mother will live with your brother every other week. I've also decided I want to be paid for taking care of her. Since you now have control of her bank accounts, you can pay me."

"Then Joey and Louise will also get paid."

"Those son-of-a-bitches won't get anything. They don't deserve it."

"But it's only fair, and having my mother live with Joey is a hardship on him. He has three young kids to support, and he doesn't make that much money."

"I didn't tell him to have all those kids, it's not my fault. Let him get another job if he can't afford to keep your mother, or let Louise get a job. It's about time she gets off her fat ass. You will not pay them to keep your mother."

"Why should you get paid but Joey and Louise not get paid? That isn't fair."

Delilah stood directly in front of Mike, staring at him. "I'm not interested in what's fair. I'm only interested in getting paid. I take her to the doctor. I get her prescriptions filled. I file her Medicare. I monitor her medications. I monitor her bank account. I do everything with no help from you or anyone. I expect to be paid or I'm walking, then you can care for your mother by yourself. See who will help you. No one, that's who."

"Okay, we'll work something out."

Two days later, Joey called Mike. "Louise had to buy some supplies for Mom. With the house payment and the kids' tuition, money is tight. Since you sold Mom's house, I know she has some money in the bank. Can we use that for her supplies?"

Mike responded, "That sounds reasonable, Delilah handles Mom's accounts, let me check with her. I'll call you back."

Mike approached Delilah. "Joey would like to use my mother's money to help pay for some of her expenses. It sounds reasonable to me. Can you go the bank tomorrow and get some cash for Joey?"

"The hell with Joey. Let him pay your mother's expenses. Since I handle all of your mother's affairs, I'm the only one who deserves any payment."

"He is not asking for payment. He is only asking for my mother to pay for her own things."

21

"No," Delilah said, her hands on her hips.

"That isn't fair."

"I don't care. Who do you want, your mother and brother or me?"

"That isn't even a fair question," Mike said with disgust.

"Take it or leave it," Delilah said as a smirk crossed her face.

Chapter 4

Although Beth longed to visit her father and grandmother, she stayed away from Delilah as much as she could. After years of witnessing Delilah's behavior, she was still surprised by it and did not want to continue to witness her mother's rants. Then two weeks after Helen began living with her, Delilah phoned Beth.

"Hi Beth. Doctor Cube noticed this witch has a hernia. He said she should have surgery but it would probably kill her."

Beth didn't know that Delilah had begun to take Helen to her doctor, Doctor Cube.

"Oh my gosh! Did you talk to Daddy? What does he want to do? She can't have surgery if Doctor Cube thinks it will kill her. Is there any other option?"

"No, I haven't talked to your father, but I've

decided she will have the surgery. Hopefully it will kill her and I'll be done with her. Doctor Cube won't do the surgery, so I'll have to find someone else. He said he won't deliberately put her life at risk. I stormed out of his office. I'm done with that son-of-a-bitch."

Doctor Cube had been Delilah's family doctor for almost twenty years, and Beth suspected that through a majority of those years, he and Delilah were having an affair. She remembered when she and her six-month-old son, Jon, were with Delilah driving to visit Delilah's aunt. They pulled into the Baker's Square parking lot just off of I-294 in Lincolnwood, Illinois, when Doctor Cube appeared at Delilah's car window.

"Hi, I hoped I would see you here today. The hotel is right up the street."

"I can't today," Delilah said as she rolled her eyes and flung her head to the side, motioning towards Beth.

"The hotel has a nice restaurant, Beth. Maybe you can wait there."

"No, maybe we better make it another day. I need to get them to my aunt's house. We'll do this another time. I'll stop by your office tomorrow."

"Damn. Okay, you better."

He bent into the car window and gave Delilah a kiss on the cheek.

$\aleph$

Beth didn't know what to say to her mother's proposal to go ahead with the surgery, but she had to say something.

"You can't be serious! You can't risk her life."

"I can and I will. I've got to go now. I've got to find some sucker that will perform the surgery."

Several weeks later, after much searching, Delilah found a doctor willing to perform the surgery. Beth met Delilah at the hospital while Helen was in surgery.

"I hope that witch dies. I don't ever want to see her ugly face again."

"Mom, don't say that. You don't really mean you want Grandma to die."

"Yes I do. I can't stand that witch."

"Then why don't you let her live with Joey and Louise?"

"I won't give them the satisfaction."

"But, Mom, it's not about who gets satisfaction, it's about what's best for Grandma."

"What's best for that witch is that she dies."

Just then the nurse entered Helen's room. "Your mother-in-law is out of surgery. Everything went well. She should be out of recovery in about an hour. I'll bring her back here to her room then."

"Oh, thank you," Delilah said, her voice dripping with concern. I was so worried about her. I'm glad everything went okay. Thank you."

Beth was stunned at Delilah's response. After the

nurse left, Delilah turned to Beth, "Son-of-a-bitch. That witch is still alive. Now she'll have to come back home with me. I dreamed I was at her funeral. Son-of-a-bitch!"

"Mom, you should be glad she's alive. Imagine how sad Daddy would be if she died. Also, you would be blamed if she died. You were the only one who wanted her to have surgery."

"I don't give a shit. I still wish she were dead. Doctor Cube promised the surgery would kill her. That's the only reason I wanted her to have it. Without the surgery, the hernia may have grown and caused that witch pain and suffering. That would have been better than what she has now. Now she'll live pain-free."

Beth was heartbroken to hear her mother's words. She didn't want to listen anymore. She loved her grandma and couldn't bear to hear what her mother was saying.

"I'm going for a walk, Mom. I'll be back in a little while."

Beth walked the halls until she saw the nurse returning Helen to her room. As she entered Helen's room, she saw Delilah bend over and kiss Helen on the forehead.

"Oh Helen, I'm so glad everything went well. I'm glad you're okay. I would have felt horrible if anything happened to you."

The nurse looked at Beth then Delilah. "I wish all my patients had such loving family members. Helen is lucky to have you for her daughter-in-law. You take such good care of her."

"It's my pleasure. I love caring for her."

Again, Beth was stunned. Although she had seen both of these sides of her mother for many years, it still surprised her each time.

A few minutes later the nurse came back in with some medication. Delilah approached the nurse. "I'll give her that. You're busy with other patients. Helen sometimes fights taking her medication. It might take a while."

"Sure, thanks. I'll be back later to make sure she took them. We don't want her to get an infection."

As the nurse left, Delilah turned to Beth. "Like hell we don't. Maybe if she gets an infection, it will kill the son-of-a-bitch."

Beth went for another walk. She could not stand to watch her mother mistreat Helen while convincing others that she provided excellent care. Such hypocrisy. When she returned, she asked Delilah about the medication. Delilah grabbed her purse and opened it. She pulled out a plastic baggie with several pills inside.

"What's that?"

"That's all the medications they brought in since she first arrived. I haven't given her anything. The only medication she has gotten was just before surgery, when I couldn't convince them to let me give it to her." Delilah returned the baggie to her purse.

"You can't do that. She needs her medication."

"I don't care. She won't get it from me."

The nurse returned with the dinner tray. "Did she take her medication?"

"Yes, it was a struggle, but she took it."

"Good. Here's her dinner. Let me know if she needs anything else."

"Okay, I will. Thank you." The nurse turned and left the room.

"What she needs is to drop dead. I'm hungry. Let's see what kind of slop they brought. Then Delilah proceeded to eat all of Helen's dinner.

"What crap. They call this dinner; it's only broth and Jell-O."

When the nurse returned, she looked at the dinner tray. "Looks like she ate everything."

"Yes, she did."

Helen looked at the nurse. "I'm hungry."

"Helen, you just finished all of your dinner. I'll bring you a snack later."

"I'm hungry."

"I'll be back later."

Beth looked at Delilah and saw an evil smirk on her face.

"Thank you, nurse," Delilah said.

"I'm going to leave now, Mom. Goodbye Grandma. I love you. See you tomorrow."

As Beth left, she approached Helen's nurse. "It might be helpful to my grandma if someone stayed in her room through her meals and also while she took her medications. Can I hire an aide to sit in her room?"

"I don't know what you mean. Your mother is in there giving Helen great care."

"I would like an aide to sit in Grandma's room," Beth said, not backing down. "How soon can you get someone? I would also like to pay for another dinner for Grandma and have someone stay with her while she eats. Please see that it happens."

"I still don't understand, but I'll see what I can do."

"Thank you. I'll be back in the morning."

When Beth returned in the morning, Delilah was already there.

"You're here early," Beth said.

"Yeah, I spent the night. I had all I could do not to smother the son-of-a-bitch with her pillow. The doctor was here early this morning. They're sending her home today. There was some volunteer here last night and this morning. She said she was training and wanted to observe Helen. She fed Helen and gave her some medication. She'll never die that way."

Just then the nurse came in with discharge papers. "It looks like you spent the night."

"Yes, I wanted to stay with Helen to make sure she was all right. I sure don't want anything to happen to her."

"I was surprised how much dinner she ate last night for the volunteer. I had thought she would have been full after eating all of the first meal I brought in."

"She has always had a big appetite."

29

Delilah stood up and stretched. "I'm so stiff from sleeping or attempting to sleep here all night."

"Are you hungry? I don't think you've left Helen's room since she returned from surgery."

"No, I'll eat when I get home. Helen's care is all that matters. I'm so tired. I didn't get any sleep."

"I'm sure you'll be glad to get home."

The nurse turned to leave. Glancing at Beth, she gave her a quick wink and whispered "thank you."

Beth nodded in response. She helped get Helen out of bed and dressed.

As they were leaving, Delilah turned to Beth. "I hoped I would be planning her funeral instead of taking her home."

Chapter 5

After Helen recovered from her surgery, she began wandering around Mike and Delilah's home. Helen had spent most of her life caring for her husband and children, as well as for her own mother. The only thing Helen knew how to do was cook, clean, and provide loving, kind nurturing to those around her. As her dementia took further hold, these attributes began to show themselves more and more. It drove Delilah crazy and she took it out on Helen. Each time they would visit one another, Delilah would brag to Louise and Beth how easy it was to be abusive to Helen.

Beth knew she needed to try and do something, so she decided to pay Helen a visit. When Delilah was out of the room, helping Helen to the bathroom, Beth saw the opportunity to talk to her father.

"Dad, please move Grandma into a nursing home. Mom came over a couple days ago to brag about slapping Grandma when Grandma tries to wipe the table. Grandma started to cry, of course, and the more Grandma cried, the more Mom would hit her. Please, Dad, it's not safe for Grandma to live with her."

"I know, Beth, I've seen bruises, but your mother won't let me move her. Every time I bring up the subject, your mother starts her ranting, threatening to leave me. She says it will cost too much money to put Grandma in a nursing home, and she won't allow it."

"We have to do something. I'm afraid Mom will really hurt Grandma someday."

"I agree but I just don't know what to do. If your mother leaves, who will take care of Grandma?"

"I'll help you, Dad, and I'm sure Louise will too. She feels as bad as I do about the way Mom treats Grandma."

"You both have young children. It would be a hardship for both of you."

"Louise already has Grandma every other week. We can alternate just like she is doing with Mom. We'll make it work."

"I don't know, Beth. You know your mother. I don't know what she might be capable of. I'm afraid if I say something, she'll take it out on you and Louise or even Grandma. I don't want any of you to be hurt."

"I know, Dad, but we have to do something."

"I'll think about it, Beth. I'll call you after I talk to her."

Beth knew that her father would have little chance of convincing Delilah to move Helen into a nursing home, even though Helen needed more and more care. When Beth returned home, she decided to contact social services and ask for their help. She was directed to a social worker by the name of Carla Rogers. Carla told Beth that, "Unless the abuse is actually witnessed by me, there is nothing I can do; it is only hearsay."

Even with repeated calls to Carla and complaints about how her grandmother was being treated, it seemed nothing could be done.

It took about two weeks, but Ms. Roger's finally did listen to Beth and called Delilah to question her. Of course, Delilah denied all allegations, convincing Carla that she did her best to provide exceptional care for Helen. Carla was convinced that Delilah provided excellent care and refused to listen to Beth any further.

Two weeks later, Louise telephoned Beth.

"I contacted social services today. I hoped if we both voiced our concerns, someone would listen. I told Carla about your grandmother's bruises just like you did and was told that since Grandma is so frail, it's easy for her to bruise. She refused to do anything. She said that she had spoken to your mother and that she is convinced that your mother provides quality care. I don't know what else to do."

"Thank you for trying, Louise. I talked to my dad about putting Grandma into a nursing home, but he's afraid of what my mother would do. What do you think about you and Joey taking her to a nursing home during the week that she's with you? You would feel my mother's scourge, but at least Grandma would be safe. I'll do whatever I can to help you."

"Joey and I had this same conversation, and we've lined up a few homes to look at. We thought if we could find a good nursing home before your grandma came back here, we could have her admitted before your mother found out. I'm sure we would feel her wrath, but that's a small price to pay for your grandmother's safety."

A few weeks later Joey and Louise did put Helen in a nursing home. When Delilah found out, she immediately removed her, bringing Helen back to her home. After she returned home with Helen, she phoned Louise.

"I brought the witch back to my house. You had no right to put her in a nursing home without my permission, now you get to pay all of the nursing home expenses. Mike and I won't pay anything and neither will Helen. You did this, you can pay. It'll be a cold day in hell before she lives with you again."

Much to everyone's dismay, the abuse continued, so Beth would drop by Mike and Delilah's house as often as she could to check on Helen's well-being.

One brisk autumn Saturday morning when Beth was visiting, she noticed Mike had a black eye. Beth questioned her father about his bruise.

"Your mother did this," he told her, "during one of our arguments. Grandma became upset because we were getting pretty loud, and she began to cry. That upset your mother more and she began to hit me, while screaming, 'She's your mother, you stupid asshole. Do something with her. You take care of her. I'm done.' When Grandma saw Delilah hit me, she became even more upset and started crying louder and harder. Your mother went into a rage and began to hit Grandma. I stepped between Grandma and your mother and then she hit me harder, while cursing at the top of her lungs. I turned away from your mother, putting my arm around Grandma's shoulder and walked her into the bedroom. I laid her down on her bed, calmed her down, and left, closing the door behind me. Delilah was still angry, so she started slapping and kicking me."

"I'm sorry dad. I just don't know what to do anymore. I tried calling social services but Mom has them convinced that she doesn't do anything wrong. I don't know what else to do or where else to turn for help. If Mom won't let you place Grandma somewhere else, I fear there is nothing we can do or no one who will help us." A tear slowly dropped from Beth's eye. "I am so sorry

Grandma has to go through this, and I'm sure it breaks your heart watching your mother suffer this abuse."

"You have no idea, Beth." Mike sat down in a kitchen chair and started wringing his hands. "I can't sleep or eat. I feel so bad for my mother. I promised my dad I would watch out for her. I can't keep my promise to my dad; I can't help my mother; I can't stand it." Beth sat down next to him and put her hand on his arm.

"I'm sorry for you too, Beth," Mike said, putting his hand on top of Beth's. "You have your own family to care for. Grandma should not be your concern, but I know how much you love her."

"I love you too, Dad. I can only imagine how bad you feel," she said, squeezing his arm. "My heart breaks for both you and Grandma. Don't worry about me. I just wish there was something I could do to stop Mom from hurting Grandma."

"I know, Beth, so do I."

א

A few months later, about a year after Helen's hernia surgery, while all of the windows in Mike and Delilah's home were open, one of the neighbors overheard Delilah's screams. They were worried and called the police. When the police arrived, the front door was open, and the police looked in through the locked screen door. What they saw was Delilah beating Mike. They asked Mike to allow them in, which he did. They told Mike that what they had witnessed gave Mike cause to file a complaint. Delilah again began to scream at Mike, telling him, "If you file a complaint, I will leave you forever, and you will have no one to care for your mother. You'll have to send her away to an institution where she would most likely be abused."

Delilah convinced Mike not to press charges, and she was left once again to continue to abuse Helen.

א

As Helen's dementia progressed, she began to have bouts of insomnia. Delilah telephoned Beth to complain.

"She walks around the house all day imagining that she's cleaning. She pisses me off. I scream at her, telling her that she is filthy and should not touch any of my things. When I slap her, she cries so I slap her even more. The more I slap her, the more upset this witch becomes."

Beth sat hard in a chair, stunned at Delilah's words.

"She gets herself so worked up, to the point that she's can't sleep. She gets out of bed and walks through the house. Then she starts to cry, calling out for her mommy. Her *mommy* has been dead almost twenty years. How am I supposed to get any sleep?"

"I scream at your father, but his only response is that there isn't anything we can do about it. The hell there isn't, I told him."

37

"Two nights ago I got up, threw Helen back in bed, closed the door, and yelled at her to stay in bed. I told her that if she gets out again, I'll beat her. If she thinks I hit her before, she hasn't seen anything yet."

"She doesn't know what she's doing, Mom. Her mind works like a little child's," Beth said, trying to reason with her mother.

"But all she does is cry, 'Mama, help me, Mama.' I tell her, 'Your mama is dead, you stupid ass. Shut up and stay in bed or you'll be sorry.'"

"She cried even louder after I said that, but I just told the stupid son-of-a bitch to shut up and I went to bed."

"Last night, the same thing happened. I had enough, so I went to the basement and rummaged around until I found what I was looking for. I asked her in a sweet voice to lie down. I decided that maybe if I didn't yell, it would be easier to get this witch to do what I wanted, at least for that night. I put the witch back to bed and tied her wrists and ankles to the bed, then I closed and locked the door behind me."

Beth felt sick to her stomach. She wasn't sure she could listen to much more, but Delilah wasn't done.

"The witch began to cry that she was scared and hurt and again started calling out for her mama. She even began to shake her bed, trying to break loose of the ropes. Her crying and the noise of the bed banging against the wall really pissed me off, so I went back into the witch's bedroom, slapped her, and told her to shut up and go to sleep."

Beth didn't know what to say, so she didn't say anything.

↘

Delilah continued to call Beth month after month complaining about Helen's insomnia. She told Beth that she finally got some sleeping pills from Doctor Cube and now "the witch" would finally sleep most of the night.

↘

One afternoon as Beth was caring for her three children, Delilah telephoned again. She was anxious to share her proud accomplishment with Beth. It was the middle of January, and the day began cold and snowy; in fact, that January was one of the coldest on record. The district had closed the schools, so Beth's children were home. Beth loved snow days. They provided extra time for her to spend with her children. She had prepared their favorite lunch – homemade mac and cheese, with extra cheese – and they were lying around on the family room floor, with a fire roaring in the fireplace.

As Delilah began her story, Beth decided to tape record the conversation.

"Once again the witch is walking through the house

wiping everything with her filthy hand. I got angry with her and began to scream and slap her. Since she's not been sleeping well lately, she became more upset than usual. She began to cry hysterically and the bitch wet her pants. That got me really pissed. Now not only do I have to contend with her routine wiping, I also have to change and wash her clothes and wash her up too. I was so angry that I actually started to shake. That made me overheat, so I turned the heat down in the house. I took your grandmother into the bathroom and stripped her totally naked. I turned the cold water on in the sink and grabbed a washcloth out of the closet. Of course, she started crying again because she said I was handling her too roughly. And when I began to wash her scrawny body, she started crying even louder."

Beth covered her mouth with her hand, afraid of what she might say to her mother. Delilah just continued her horrible tale.

"Her cries became louder and louder, so I hit her in the mouth with the back of my hand. The dumb bitch was still wet so she stumbled over the bathtub and hit the back of her head against the wall. That made her cry even louder and uncontrollably. I got her out of the tub and threw her naked body onto the back porch, locking the door behind me. Now that gave her something to cry about."

"Is she still outside?" Beth said, trying to keep her hands from shaking.

"Damn right. It's where she deserves to be. She can stay out there until she freezes to death. I won't have to care for her if she drops dead. I won't have to listen to her calling for her mama every night, the stupid ass."

"Bring her back inside!" Beth yelled. "You need to dry her off and get her dressed." Beth thought quickly, trying to figure out what to say to Delilah that wouldn't upset her but would convince her to bring Helen back inside. "If she gets sick, you'll have more to do to care for her."

"If I don't bring her in, maybe she'll die."

"Then there will be an investigation," Beth pressed. "Social services already has you on their radar. And remember the police report? You don't want any further scrutinizing. It isn't worth it. Bring her inside right now!"

Beth didn't hear anything for a moment except Delilah's breathing. "You're right," she finally said. "They would make it sound like it's all my fault. Nobody would think she went out on the cold porch all naked and wet by herself. Okay, I'll bring her in."

Delilah hung up, and Beth sat down and began to cry.

It was the middle of the afternoon, so Beth was home alone with her three children. She was without a vehicle, so she knew she wouldn't be able to take Helen away from her mother to protect her. She decided she had to call her father at work.

"Dad, I just talked to Mom. I'm shaking I'm so

angry with her. She hit Grandma and made her fall into the bathtub. Then while Grandma was wet and cold, Mom put her out onto the cold porch. I'm afraid for Grandma. Mom needs psychiatric help. Without proper intervention, Grandma will be seriously injured someday. Dad, you have to get Mom some help."

"Beth, I don't know what to do."

"I tape recorded the conversation I had with Mom today. I will use it if I need to. I'll call the authorities and Grandma will be removed from your house and Mom will go to jail for abusing Grandma. You need to convince my mother to get help."

"I'll see what I can do."

Chapter 6

At Mike's insistence and with the knowledge that the conversation Beth had with her mother about putting Helen out on the cold porch was tape recorded, Delilah had decided to contact Doctor Cube and discuss the situation with him. Beth was visiting to check in on Helen when Delilah called the doctor.

"Bob, this is Delilah. Helen has gotten me so upset. She wet herself, and while I was washing her, she fell and hit her head. I was so worried about her. I put her on the enclosed back porch, where I believed she couldn't hurt herself. While she was out there, I called Beth. I told Beth what happened, and she got upset with me. I don't know why."

Delilah turned her stony gaze toward Beth. "She

called Mike and gave him some bullshit story that I was mean to Helen. I treat Helen well. No other daughter-in-law would do all I do for that witch. Nobody appreciates all I do for Helen. Now they both are insisting I get mental help. Maybe, they're right. That woman gets me so angry."

"Maybe what you need is a break from Helen. Let me see what I can do. I can probably get you admitted. I'll keep you in the hospital for several days so you can get a good rest."

"Yeah, let Mike deal with his mother. Maybe then he'll appreciate all I do. He'll see all the trouble she causes me."

"I'll have to see you in my office first. When can you get here?"

Delilah put the phone down. "I need you to watch Grandma this afternoon. I have a doctor's appointment."

"I have to pick the kids up from school, Mom. I can't."

"You and that bastard husband of mine want me to get help but you can't even watch your grandmother for a couple of hours. Some daughter you are."

Delilah stood up and turned away from Beth.

"I'll have to get Helen dressed and see if Louise will take her. My deadbeat daughter can't watch her for me. I haven't spoken to Louise since she tried putting Helen in a nursing home so she is probably mad at me."

"I hope she will take her. You haven't been here in

a while. It will be good to see you alone. You'll have to come to my office for a pre-admitting physical. When can I expect you?

"Between two and four. I'd like to be back home before Mike gets home from work, then he'll see how hard I go out of my way. He'll see what a good wife I am."

"Okay, see you this afternoon."

Later that week Doctor Cube had Delilah committed to a psychiatric unit of St. Luke's Hospital. While Delilah was in the hospital, Beth went to visit. Delilah told Beth that the nurses had given her a written psychological evaluation questionnaire to complete. Delilah began to go down the list of questions, reading them to Beth.

"Beth, help me answer these questions. I don't want anyone to think I'm crazy."

Beth shook her head. "I can't answer questions for you. You have to answer them yourself."

"But if I answer them, they may think I'm crazy. They won't think I'm crazy with your answers."

"No, you have to answer them yourself. If they think you have a problem, they can help you."

"There's nothing wrong with me, you son-of-a-bitch. If you're not here to help me, then you might as well leave." Delilah lay in bed with her hands on her hips and her back arched.

"Of course I'm here to help you. I just won't answer your questions for you. I'm here to assure you get whatever help you need. I know Grandma is a burden."

"You know? How the hell do you know? How does anyone know? I'm the only one who is with that witch twenty-four seven. I don't get any help from anyone. I have to do everything myself."

"Joey and Louise are willing to help. In fact, isn't Grandma there now, so you can have a break?"

"Joey and Louise can go to hell. You can all go to hell. I'm the only one that provides proper care for that witch. Joey and Louise don't care for her the way I do. All they want to do is spend money and put her in a home. I won't put her in a home. They better not put her in a home while I'm in here or there will be hell to pay."

Delilah became enraged and began to scream so loudly that it hurt Beth's ears. She was throwing her arms in the air and shaking her finger at Beth. A nurse came in to Delilah's room to find out why she was screaming.

"My daughter is speaking meanly to me, and she is getting me so upset."

"Maybe you better leave now. Your mother is quite upset."

"Sure, it's probably best."

Beth turned back towards Delilah. "I'll call you tomorrow to see if you need anything."

"What I need is for you to go to hell. I needed you to help me today but you refused to help. You don't do anything to help me; nobody does anything to help me."

As Beth turned to leave, she noticed the nurse rolling her eyes at Delilah. "Thanks, Beth," the nurse said.

"Sure. I'll call you tomorrow, Mom. Have a good night."

Two days later Delilah telephoned Beth to ask if she could take her home. When Beth arrived, she heard the nurse talking to Delilah.

"Here are your prescriptions. The doctor wants you to get them filled on your way home and begin taking them today. Here are the names of some psychiatrists. You need to follow up with one of them. The doctor believes you would benefit from long-term counseling. Do you have any questions?"

"No, thank you."

"Beth, do you have any questions?"

Beth turned toward the nurse

"Let me get this straight. Mom will need to be on medications. How long will that be needed, and how long should she anticipate needing to see a counselor?"

"It's hard to say with certainty; however, she may need them both for the rest of her life."

"Should we make other arrangements for my grandma's care?"

"That might be best."

"Thanks. Okay, Mom, are you ready to go?" Beth asked as she picked up her mother's overnight bag.

"Yes, and thank you, nurse."

"You're welcome. Is there anything else either of you need?"

"No, thank you," Delilah answered.

The nurse turned toward Beth. "Anything else you need?"

"No thanks. I have your phone number if my dad or I have any other questions. Thanks for taking good care of my mom."

"You're welcome, and thanks to you too, Beth."

The nurse walked out the door. Beth turned to see Delilah tearing the paperwork the nurse had given her. "Thank you for taking good care of your mom," Delilah said in a mocking tone. "They treated me like they thought I was crazy. Son-of-a-bitches, I don't need any damn shrink or any damn medication. They're the ones who are nuts, not me."

"Mom, you should not have done that," Beth said in frustration. "You've been in this hospital for almost a week. The doctor has had plenty of time to decide what is best for you. Maybe if you take his advice, you'll start to feel better."

"I feel fine. Everyone can go to hell. I don't need any help. All I need is for your asshole grandmother to quit aggravating me."

"That can be solved."

"I will not allow her to go into a nursing home. I won't spend her money. I deserve that money for putting up with her all of these years."

"Then let her live with Joey and Louise."

"No. Let's go."

Beth felt sick on the drive to Delilah's house. Her

efforts to get her mother help were in vain. She believed that without her mother seeking intervention, the abuse to Helen would continue.

Chapter 7

During the time Delilah was in the hospital, Helen stayed with Joey and Louise. Beth phoned to see how Louise was coping.

"Your grandma is calm, happy, and has a ravenous appetite. Joey remarked at what a difference there has been in her while she's been with us. One concern though, it doesn't seem as though your mother is giving me all of the medication your grandma is supposed to be taking. Your mother told me she gives Helen tranquilizers and sleeping pills, yet I don't have those, although, I would not have needed them. Your grandma has been easy for me to care for."

"I don't know anything about Grandma's medications. I'll give Dad a call and see if he knows. I'll call you right back.

Beth hung up the phone and called Mike.

"Your mother maintains control over Helen's medications. She doesn't even let me see her prescription bottles. Doctor Cube also provides samples of medications, so nobody but the doctor and your mother know what the doctor has given Helen or, more specifically, has given Delilah to use at will."

ℵ

When Delilah returned home from the hospital, she demanded that Helen be returned back to her.

Beth questioned her mother. "Mom, do you really think that's a good idea? The nurse suggested you take some time away from Grandma. Maybe you should let her stay with Louise a few more days."

"Go to hell. She is coming home; I don't care what anyone says. Who knows what the hell they're doing to her over there."

"Louise is taking good care of Grandma; I speak to her several times a day. Grandma is always happy, and she loves being with the kids. She'll be fine for a few more days."

"Louise just wants Helen to stay with her so she can control the situation."

"I'm sure that's not true. Louise only wants to make things easier for you, and she enjoys Grandma's company."

"She only wants to make things easier for herself.

She'll tell everyone, just like she tells you, what a great job she's doing with Helen. She thinks everyone will feel sorry for her and all that just boosts her ego."

"Louise doesn't have time to play games. She's busy with three kids and Uncle Joey. I believe she genuinely cares for Grandma."

"See, she has you fooled."

Beth shook her head. It was hard for her to not lose patience with her mother. "No Mom, she doesn't have me fooled. I've seen her with Grandma, and I speak to her often. I would sense a problem if there was one."

"I don't care what anyone says, that witch will come back here today."

"Louise doesn't think Grandma is a witch. Maybe you should leave her there a few more days."

"No."

א

Delilah kept calling Joey and Louise, insisting they bring Helen back to her house. She told Louise that she would call social services and tell them they were holding Helen against her will and that Helen wanted to return to her but Joey and Louise refused to bring her back. No one saw a way around Delilah, so they eventually gave in to her demand.

After Joey brought Helen back to Mike and Delilah's home, Helen again began to get upset, cry, lose her appetite, and suffer from insomnia, so Delilah started abusing her again. She would brag to Beth how easy it was to do because everyone was either afraid of her or, as in the case of social services, thought she provided excellent care. She told Beth and Louise point blank, "If either of the two of you ever calls social services again, I will tell them you are both just trying to make me look bad because you don't want them to know that you are both bad mothers. I've convinced social services that I'm innocent of accusations made by both of you, and I have convinced them that I am a good person. They would believe me if I made accusations against you. Your children would be taken away from you and given to me."

This made Louise and Beth afraid for their children and apprehensive about reporting Delilah.

The entire family understood that Delilah created fear in everyone she encountered. Fear was the operative word for Delilah. Everyone was afraid of what Delilah might say about them to others or what she might do to get even with them if they angered her. She had a way of distorting the truth, especially if it served her purpose. People were afraid to get on her "bad side." They knew if they did, she would gossip about them, probably saying things that were not true. Then she would try to convince others to sever any relationships with the person she had become angry with. Everyone close to Delilah knew she was not to be taken lightly.

Chapter 8

Beth visited Delilah often to check on Helen. On one of those visits, Delilah told Beth that she had gone to a funeral home to ask exactly what had to be done if a person died in another person's home.

"The funeral director told me that if Helen dies at home, I have to call the police, but if she has seen Doctor Cube within three days of her death, I can just call the undertaker."

"Why do you need to know that? Grandma is fine. Doctor Cube said Grandma should live for a long time. She is strong and healthy, except for her dementia."

"I've been buying a lot of medication books and looking up side effects of her medications. Some of her medication can have deadly consequences if she takes too much or if they are mixed together. I just want to be prepared."

"Well, if you know the potential harm of her medications, then you know what not to mix and what amount she should be given so she won't overdose."

"I just want to be prepared. I also researched what signs to look for to assure someone is dying." Delilah smirked as she clapped her hands together.

"Mom, that's morbid and ridiculous. Grandma is healthy, and you can monitor her medication. Nothing will happen to her."

"You never know."

Just then, Helen began to cry for her Mama. Delilah's response shocked Beth.

"Shut up you son-of-a-bitch or I will shut you up permanently."

"Mom, don't say that."

"Why not, I mean it, and don't tell me to let her live with Joey and Louise or put her in a home. I will never do that. I'll kill her before I do that."

"Mom, stop."

"I've had it. She's always calling for her mama. Her mother has been dead twenty years."

"Mom, she has dementia; she doesn't know any better. You have to be patient with her."

"I'll be patient. I'll kill the son-of-a-bitch."

Beth could no longer tolerate listening to her mother.

"Mom, I've got to go. Bye, Grandma, I'll be back soon."

On the way home, Beth wondered what she could do to protect Helen without putting her children at risk. When Beth got home, she called Carla Rogers at social services again to relay her conversation with her mother.

"My mom is threatening to kill my grandma. I'm afraid for my grandma. My mother is not taking the psych meds she was prescribed in the hospital. She is fixated on death and dying and she is threatening to have my children taken away if I say anything to you. Please help me help my grandma."

"Nobody can force your mother to take her meds," Carla said, a note of irritation in her voice. "As I've told you before, our investigation didn't turn up anything. We have no concerns. Your mother is probably just stressed today. There is nothing we can do."

"What's going to happen when she get so stressed she acts on her threats and kills my grandma?"

There was a brief moment of silence before Carla responded. "Let's just hope that doesn't happen. Again, there is nothing we can do."

Once again, Beth felt frustrated and helpless. It appeared there was nothing she could do to help Helen. As she hung up the phone she sat down and cried.

א

The following week Louise called Beth.

"Hi Beth. Your mother called to ask me to keep your grandma while she went to an appointment and she just dropped her off. Joey and I are both shocked at the condition your grandma was in. Your dad carried Helen in because she could not walk. She appears to be semi-comatose. We need to do something."

"Oh my gosh, Louise, what did you do? Did you ask why Grandma was in that condition?"

"Yes. Your mother said she believed the new medication Doctor Cube prescribed was probably too strong. She said she would follow up with him tomorrow."

"Tomorrow, what about today? Maybe you should take her to the emergency room."

"I mentioned that to your mother. She began to scream at me. She said she would deal with it tomorrow and that I should mind my own business."

"But Grandma is your business."

"I know, Beth. I just don't know what to do. Joey is going crazy too. We're just so afraid of what your mother might do if we report her. We doubt if anyone would even listen to us. You know how she managed to get social services on her side."

"I agree, but I'm so afraid for Grandma. How is she doing now?"

"She cannot be roused; she just stays asleep on the couch where your dad placed her. She won't even eat or drink, not even for the kids."

"That's terrible. I'll let you go so you can continue to monitor her. I'll call you tonight. In the meantime, call me if you need anything"

"Okay. Thanks, Beth, I will."

א

Later that evening, Beth had just finished putting her children to bed when the telephone rang.

"Hi, Beth. Do you have time to talk?"

"Yes, I just finished putting the boys down for the night. What happened when my parents came back to pick up Grandma?"

"Your mother walked in all cocky and arrogant. Your dad kept his head down, looking sad and just walked over to Helen, picked her up, and carried her to the car. Your mother asked if I had anything to report. I said no, and she started to walk out the door. She stopped, turned to look at me with those evil eyes, and said, 'When Helen gets home, she'll get proper care.'"

Louise began to cry.

"Don't cry, Louise. You know she's just trying to get to you. We both need to stay strong for Grandma and for my dad and Joey, too."

"I give her proper care."

"I know you do. Let's just hope my mother calls Doctor Cube tomorrow and hope he will help Grandma.

I don't know what else we can do. Thank you for taking good care of Grandma. My dad, Joey, and I all appreciate it. Keep strong."

"I'll try. Thanks for your encouragement."

"You're welcome. Now, try to get a good night sleep. I'll talk to you tomorrow."

"Thanks, Beth. Goodnight."

"Goodnight. Talk to you tomorrow.

א

Over the next few weeks Delilah and Louise again started sharing the responsibility of Helen's care. One of the days Helen was with Delilah, Beth stopped in. She didn't even have her coat off when Delilah began her rant.

"I can't tolerate this witch anymore. I asked Doctor Cube for stronger tranquilizers for her. Yesterday, I gave her the new tranquilizer with her sleeping pill and I didn't have a problem with her at all. Maybe, I'll do the same today."

"Mom, you can't mix her medication. That's dangerous."

"I don't give a shit. I can't tolerate her anymore."

"I'll stay here all day with you. I'll leave when the kids are coming home from school. You will only have one hour until Daddy gets home. You can tolerate her for one hour. I'll try to come over more. Maybe Louise can come over too. We'll work together."

"I don't want that son-of-a-bitch Louise here."

"Okay, I'll just try to come over more."

Beth telephoned Louise when she returned home and told her about her conversation with Delilah.

"I know, she told me the same thing. She also said that when your grandma is there, she fluctuates between consciousness and unconsciousness. I find it difficult to believe because when your grandmother is here, she's quite lucid."

"That is strange. Louise, maybe you should start keeping a log book. Document everything. Grandma's state of mind, level of consciousness, appetite, any bruises. Maybe if we document everything, someone may listen."

"I had the same thought. I'm going out today to buy a log book."

"Let's just keep trying to think of ways we can get help for Grandma. I think my mother is losing control. I'm afraid of what she might do."

"Me too."

א

The following week was Louise's week to care for Helen. Louise called Beth to tell her that before she brought Helen, Delilah took Helen to Doctor Cube for her annual checkup. Louise told Beth she became frightened when Delilah became enraged, telling her, "Doctor Cube again said this witch is healthy, has a strong heart, and should have many more years to live. I don't want this son-of-a-bitch to live many more years. I feel trapped. I want to be left alone. I'll never have freedom until this witch is gone."

"I told her she'd have freedom this week. If she wants, I'd keep Helen an extra week. She refused and said she'd be back next Monday to pick her up. I told her, okay but if she changes her mind, let me know. She said she won't. Beth, I'm scared."

א

A few days later Beth received a call from Delilah.

"I visited Doctor Cube to ask them how I could kill Helen so no one would suspect."

Delilah began to laugh, "Your grandma should be dead of heart failure in two weeks and no one will be able to determine why."

Beth could not believe what she was hearing. Her mother couldn't really be capable of murder. She froze. She didn't know what to do. Social services would not believe her. *Should I call the police? What can they do?*

After that telephone call, Beth called Mike and Delilah every day or she would stop by unexpectedly to make sure Helen was still okay.

א

The following week, Beth was surprised to see Helen when she went to visit Louise.

"Your mother asked that I care for your grandma. When your grandma was brought here, she was unconscious. Your mother admitted to giving her additional sleeping medication while she was in that unconscious state saying that she stuffed it into her mouth forcing her to swallow it."

Beth's jaw dropped. "You're kidding."

"I wish I was."

Together they called social services. They asked for Carla Rogers but they were told Carla was no longer with the agency."

"Is there someone else we can talk to?"

"Yes, I'll give you to Sandy Ramey."

"Hi, this is Sandy. How can I help you?"

Beth and Louise repeated the entire story of Helen's time with Delilah and the mistreatment Helen had suffered for months.

"I'm shocked there has not been any further investigation. Can I come out and talk to both of you tomorrow? I want to observe her for myself."

"Sure," Beth said. "I'll make arrangements for my kids. What time do you want me here?"

"How about ten a.m.?"

"That sounds great. Delilah is supposed to pick up

Helen tomorrow, but she's a late sleeper. She doesn't get here until afternoon."

"Okay, I'll see both of you tomorrow."

א

Before Sandy was able to come out to investigate, Delilah brought Helen back to her home. Louise telephoned Sandy.

"I can't believe Delilah was here so early. She usually sleeps until noon. I wonder if she suspected something, although I can't imagine why she would. Can you investigate at Delilah's home?"

"I can, I just need to be careful. Delilah sounds dangerous. Let me talk to my supervisor and get back to you. I still cannot believe no one from our office did a follow-up investigation. It's bizarre. I'll call you back after I've talked to my supervisor."

A few days later Sandy phoned Beth.

"My supervisor agreed to go with me to your mother's house. We hope there's security in numbers. Every time I try to call your mother to schedule an appointment, she hangs up the phone. We stopped at her house and she did not answer the door. We will keep trying. I just wanted to give you an update. Beth, please be careful. She sounds scary."

"Thanks for your efforts, Sandy. I'll be careful. You do the same."

"Thanks Beth, I will. I'll call you if I have anything to update."

א

Two days after the conversation Beth had with Sandy Ramey, Delilah called Joey.

"Your mother is dead."

She called back a few minutes later saying, "I made a mistake, she isn't really dead."

Joey and Louise fled to Helen's side. By the time they got to Delilah's home, Helen *was* dead. Delilah told Joey and Louise that she checked on Helen several times that morning, waiting for her to die. Mike wanted to call EMS but Delilah wouldn't allow him to. Delilah refused to allow anyone to call the funeral home until she had removed Helen's nightgown, washed her, and changed all of her bedding. By the time the funeral home was called, Helen's body was cold and becoming rigid.

The cause of Helen's death would be declared heart failure. The undertaker questioned Delilah, asking why she did not call for help when she knew Helen was dying. He said all she would have had to do was make one phone call to save Helen's life.

The undertaker told Joey and Beth, "It is strange that Delilah washed Helen and all of her bedding before calling. The only reason people wash the body or the scene before notifying anybody, is to remove evidence. I also think it's strange that Delilah did not shed a tear, did not show any remorse. She was cold as stone."

ℵ

Helen's body was transported to Johnston, Wisconsin where she had spent much of her life. Delilah made sure that she was the center of attention at Helen's wake. She stood stone-faced until someone approached her. Then she began to sob, stating how much she missed Helen, how lonely it was going to be without her, and what good care she took of Helen while she was alive. Beth, Joey, and Louise just looked at each other in disbelief.

Helen was buried in the town's cemetery next to her husband Sam and close to her parents.

Most of Helen's estate went to Mike, or rather Delilah. Joey received very little. After the burial, when he questioned Mike, Delilah answered, "Be glad you have anything. I was the only one that took care of Helen; therefore, I should be the one to receive her entire estate."

Joey realized he would not get anywhere arguing with Delilah.

Delilah was finally happy...if only temporarily.

Chapter 9

Two weeks after Helen died, Delilah's mother, Margaret, was diagnosed with cancer. Beth spent much of her childhood with Margaret. When Beth was a toddler, Delilah and Mike lived in an apartment that did not allow children. Before that, Delilah would leave Beth with Margaret for days at a time, because Beth was an inconvenience, so Beth was raised by her grandmother for the first four years of her life. Later, Beth spent several summers living with Margaret because Delilah felt she would have more freedom without having Beth around. Beth and Margaret were so close that at times, they would finish each other's sentences. Margaret had shown Beth a love that she never felt from Delilah, and

Beth showed her grandmother the love Delilah had never showed Margaret.

Margaret's mother emigrated from London, England in her teenage years. Her father emigrated from Dublin, Ireland, also as a teenager. They both settled in Chicago where they met and married. It was a beautiful wedding: high Victorian, gay nineties style. They were a beautiful couple. Together they had five children. Margaret was the middle of those children, born at the dawn of the new century. She was raised in a loving, caring home in proper Victorian manner.

Margaret had a great love of life, and she lived with a happy, cheerful disposition. She was a beautiful child, with blonde ringlets falling around her shoulders and clear, blue-gray eyes. Margaret had a natural grace coupled with her beauty; she was always the belle of the ball. All of the young men flocked to her, hoping for a dance or better yet, a courting. It was at one of those balls that she lost her heart to a tall, handsome, dark-haired fireman.

Margaret was eighteen when they married. While the twenties were roaring in Chicago, Margaret bore six children, five boys with the daughter, Debbie, in the middle.

Chicago was a major industrial center, factories were poking up everywhere. Along with factories came smoke and pollution. When Debbie was just eight years old, it was believed that pollution caused Debbie to contract lung cancer. After Debbie died, Margaret's marriage fell apart. Margaret was left alone with five sons to raise.

She began working in one of those factories she believed was responsible for taking Debbie's life. She was growing older but was still a great beauty. A handsome, middle-aged man by the name of Joe Bawlder was smitten. He had moved to Chicago and began working at the factory two weeks before Margaret. After three months of dating, they were married. He became a father to Margaret's five children, while they had two daughters of their own, Bertha and Delilah.

Delilah had been doted on and pampered by her parents and all of her siblings throughout her life. Delilah learned to be self-centered and demanding. She believed the whole world revolved around her.

After Joe died, Delilah believed that, as the youngest child, she should make all decisions concerning Margaret's care. While Beth was visiting Margaret, as she did every Wednesday, Margaret's youngest son, Norman, also came to visit. Beth thought this was unusual.

Margaret and Beth were sitting in the living room, Margaret on the sofa, Beth in the large overstuffed chair, when the doorbell rang. Beth rose to answer the door, and her Uncle Norman stepped in.

"Hi Beth."

"Hi, Uncle Norman. This is a surprise. What are you doing here; shouldn't you be at work?"

"I'm on my lunch break. I wanted to come today because I knew you would be here. I am hoping for your support."

Beth had a puzzled look on her face. "My support, why do you need my support?"

Norman walked into the living room. "Hi Mom," Norman said, then he walked over to the front window and rested his elbow on the high windowsill. He began to bite his bottom lip. "Mom, Marie and I have decided you should not live alone. Cancer is scary. You may need a lot of care. It will be easier on everyone if you don't live alone. Then no one will have to schedule their time to come to check on you. Marie agreed, you can live with us."

Margaret began tapping her fingers on the arm of the sofa. "I don't know Norman, I don't want to be a burden, and Marie sometimes doesn't feel well herself."

Norman walked over to his mother. "It'll be fine. I talked to the rest of the family. Everyone is willing to help out. You can stay with one of your other children if Marie needs a break. It will work out."

"I don't know. What do you think, Beth?" Beth thought for a moment, *I don't want Grandma living with my mother!*

Beth glanced at her Uncle Norman, then back at her grandma. "I think that's a good idea, Grandma." Beth looked back at Uncle Norman. She smiled to see his body relax; he was no longer biting his lip. She smiled, then

69

looked back at her grandma. "I would feel better knowing you weren't alone. I'll also help out if Aunt Marie needs a break. You can stay with Edward and me. The boys would love having you with us. I think you should do it."

"Okay, Norman, I'll do it. Are you sure it's okay with Marie?" Margaret said with a sigh.

"Yes, Mom, I'm sure. You and Marie have always been good friends. Heck, you are the one who told me to marry her."

"Yes I did and I'm glad I did."

"Okay, it's settled. Think about what you want to bring with you. Marie and I will bring our boys over Saturday morning to pack you up. It'll be great having you with us, Mom." Norman took a deep breath and exhaled. "Thanks Beth."

"Okay, Norman, I'll see you Saturday. I love you."

"I love you too, Mom. See you Saturday. Bye Beth." Norman bent down to kiss Margaret on the cheek.

Beth walked her uncle to the door. "Goodbye, Uncle Norman."

꙳

Delilah stopped by to visit Margaret later that week. Margaret was sorting through her closet, arranging piles labeled "Keep," "Toss," and "Donate." Delilah also noted a box marked "Marie."

Delilah stood directly in front of Margaret, one hand

on her hip, shaking her finger directly in Margaret's face.

"What are you doing? What are all these piles for? Why is there a box marked for Marie?"

"I'm moving in with Norman and Marie. Norman doesn't think I should live alone anymore. It will be easier for Marie to provide care for me if I'm living with her, and she won't have to drive out here every day."

Delilah's nostrils began to flare, her eyes squinted, and her body began shaking.

"Why the hell should Marie provide care? She is nothing to you. I'm your daughter. I should provide your care, not Marie."

"This will be easier for you too. You won't have to worry about driving out here every day."

"You should live with me, not Marie. I'm your youngest child. I should provide your care, not Marie," Delilah said through pursed lips.

Margaret stood erect, looking Delilah directly in the eye. "It's already settled. I'm moving in with Norman and Marie. They're bringing their boys Saturday to get me moved."

Delilah began to perspire, clenching her fists.

"Why didn't you discuss this with me first? You shouldn't make decisions without discussing it. Norman and Marie probably just want your money. That's all they ever want from you."

"I made my decision after discussing the situation

with Norman. What I do with my money is my business. Beth also thought it was a good idea."

"What the hell does Beth know? Why is there a box marked Marie?" Delilah began to sift through the box. "If you are giving anything away, you should give it to me."

"Marie always admired my knickknack cabinet. I promised her she could have some knickknacks."

Delilah picked up a porcelain dog out of the box. "I should have your knickknacks. Some of those were from my grandma."

"She was Norman's grandma too."

"I don't give a shit. You can all go to hell. Don't ask me to help you."

Delilah opened the door to leave when Margaret called to her, "Goodbye, sweetheart. I love you."

"Go to hell," Delilah said slamming the door behind her.

א

Beth went to Margaret's house on Saturday to help move her grandma. Margaret related the conversation she had with Delilah.

"Your mother is angry with me because I chose to live with Uncle Norman. She thinks I should live with her. She is mad at you too, Beth, because you agreed with us. I sure hope she doesn't take it out on you."

"Don't worry about me, Grandma. I'll be fine."

Beth forced a smile. "You know my mother has a quick, hot temper. She'll get over it."

Beth noticed Margaret's furrowed brow. "I know, but I remember the beatings she used to give you and your grandma Helen. I'm afraid to live with her."

"You made the right decision. I think you'll be happy with Aunt Marie."

"Thanks for your support, Beth." Margaret reached into her apron pocket and pulled out a small box. "I put this locket aside for you. Grandpa gave me this as an engagement present. I want you to have it."

Beth took the box and opened it. She took the locket out and gasped. "It's beautiful. Why do you want me to have it?"

"You spent so much time with me and Grandpa, first when you were a little girl and you lived with us, and after you were married, we relied on you to help us. We both loved you very much. I know Grandpa would want you to have it."

"Thank you, Grandma." Beth gave her grandma a hug. "I'll cherish it forever."

"I know you will."

As they were hugging each other, Norman and his three sons walked through the door. Norman started to laugh. "Enough hugging. Get to work."

"Yes sir, uncle dictator," Beth said with a giggle in her voice, as she saluted her uncle.

Margaret also began laughing. Beth smiled at her grandmother.

א

Beth, Norman, and Norman's three sons worked through the day to get Margaret packed and moved. On Beth's drive home, she glanced at the locket resting on the seat beside her. She began to reminisce about the time she spent with her grandparents and how sad she was when her Grandpa Joe died. She also remembered how sad she was when Grandpa Sam died and the years of abuse Grandma Helen suffered at Delilah's hand. Beth was glad her Grandma Margaret chose not to live with her mother.

Beth recalled an incident just the year before. Delilah brought Margaret to her home for lunch. It was a warm spring day and Margaret decided she would like to sit outside after lunch. As Margaret and Delilah were walking out the door, Margaret said with a sigh, "I love sitting outside, I always have. There isn't anywhere for me to sit outside at my apartment, so I'm glad that Marie brings me to her house several times a week. They have a pretty yard. I love sitting out there."

"I'm sick of hearing about Norman and Marie. Shut up talking about them." Delilah's body stiffened.

Just then Margaret fell and hurt her hip. Hours later Margaret continued to complain of the pain from her fall. Delilah smirked. "Tell Norman and Marie about your pain. Where are they now? How can they help you now?"

Margaret began to cry. "Please, Delilah, if you

won't help me, call Marie. I would like to go to the emergency room. My hip really hurts."

"Bullshit! I won't call Marie. I'll be the good child and take you," Delilah said with a sneer.

Margaret could hardly walk. She screamed in pain with each step she took. She made it to Delilah's car, and Delilah drove her to the emergency room. It was determined she had a broken hip.

Margaret was admitted to the hospital and had emergency surgery, followed by a lengthy hospital stay. As Margaret was recovering, Beth came by to visit. As she walked into the room, she noticed Margaret sitting in a recliner.

"Hi Grandma, how are you feeling? What happened? How did you fall?"

"Beth, I don't know why I fell. I was holding the railing and paid attention to where I was stepping." Margaret hesitated before continuing in a whisper. "I almost believe your mother tripped me."

"Did you tell anyone?"

"No, just you." Margaret's body stiffened.

"Maybe you should tell the nurse. At least they can write it in your chart."

Margaret tried to shift her weight off of her hip.

"Ouch. I'm afraid of what else your mother might do to me. I know how much she abuses your Grandma Helen. I don't want that."

Beth started to shake. "I don't want that either;

that's why you have to say something. We have to stop her."

"I'm too afraid."

"Grandma, if you won't say anything, I'm afraid there is nothing I can do." Beth knew that if she accused Delilah of purposefully tripping her grandmother, Delilah would convince the doctor and nurses that Beth was lying just to get her in trouble. "You'll just have to stay away from her." Beth shifted her weight back and forth, annoyed that there was nothing she could do.

"Well, Grandma, I'm going to leave so you can calm down and try to rest. Don't think about my mother. I'll be back to visit on Wednesday. If you need me, just call. You need anything before I leave?"

"Just a hug."

"My pleasure."

As Beth hugged her grandma, she heard her grandma whisper, "I love you. You're my savior."

"I love you too, Grandma. Goodbye, see you Wednesday."

As Beth turned to leave, she glanced back to give her grandma a smile and a wink. She noticed a tear trickling down her grandma's cheek. "Don't cry, Grandma. I'll be back. I love you."

Beth had to hurry out the door because she felt a tear welling in the corner of her eye and didn't want Margaret to see.

Before cancer had struck, Margaret was a sturdy woman with snow white hair. She had now become a shell of her former self. She was also less tenacious and unwilling to stand up for herself. She became dependent on Norman, Marie, and Beth to fight for her, which they all did willingly.

א

Two weeks after Margaret's move, Marie telephoned Beth and invited her and Joseph to lunch.

As Beth approached her aunt's door, she was hit in the face with the smell of freshly baked bread. Upon entering, she also smelled her aunt's famous chicken noodle soup.

Marie opened the door.

"Yummy, something smells good. I can't wait to eat."

Marie giggled. "Hello, Beth. Hello, Joseph," she said, rustling the small boy's hair.

"Hi, Aunt Marie. Hello, Grandma," Beth said and walked over to her grandmother and gave her a kiss on the cheek.

"Hi, Grandma!" Joseph said, running up to Margaret and wrapping his arms around her. "I'm a big boy now, I'm this many," he said while holding up three chubby little fingers.

Margaret chuckled. "You *are* a big boy."

"How are you feeling?" Beth asked.

"I'm doing fine, Beth. Thanks."

Marie told Beth to sit with Margaret in the living room while she finished preparing lunch. Beth pulled Joseph up on her lap but before long, he started exploring Norman and Marie's home.

"Is Uncle Norman home?" Beth asked her grandmother.

"No, he is at work."

"Darn, now I have no one to razz," Beth said with a giggle. Beth and Margaret sat on the living room sofa and watched after Joseph.

"Your mother called me yesterday. She still thinks I should stay with her because she is my baby. She really wants to take care of me," Margaret said with a sigh. "She thinks I'm a burden to Marie and that Marie may have to care for her own mother someday. I told her when Marie needs a break, I'll find somewhere to go. I have other children who are willing to keep me. Marie assures me I am not a burden."

"I'm sure you're not a burden to Aunt Marie," Beth said, squeezing her grandmother's hand.

"Then your mother said, 'Sure she says that now; she just wants you to stay with her so she can get what she wants out of you.' I told her I'm not demented; she won't get anything I don't want her to have. Of course, your mother got angry and said, 'Well, when they take everything from you and you're down on your luck, don't call me.' Then she slammed down the telephone."

"Don't let her get to you. She is just trying to get you to stay with her," Beth said to Margaret as she stood up and walked to the kitchen.

"Need any help?" she asked her Aunt Marie.

While Beth was helping Marie set the table, Margaret sat on the sofa and Joseph sat on the floor next to the coffee table as they put a puzzle together. Beth recognized the table as the one that she used to put puzzles together on while living with her grandmother. Beth was overcome with a warm sensation realizing that Joseph was the fourth generation of the family to put puzzles together on that table. The telephone rang. Marie answered.

"Hi Delilah, your mother is fine. She's playing with Joseph while Beth is helping me with lunch."

There was a lull in the conversation while Marie listened. "Okay, see you in a bit."

She rolled her eyes as she hung up the phone. "Delilah decided since you and Joseph are here, she should have been invited also. She said she will be right over, invited or not."

Margaret shuddered. "This should be fun. So much for a peaceful, enjoyable day."

Beth looked at her Aunt Marie, shaking her head. "Should I set another place?"

"I guess you have to. Yeah, so much for a peaceful, enjoyable day."

Fifteen minutes later the doorbell rang. Marie went to open the door. "Here goes nothing. Let the fun begin."

Delilah pushed the door open, knocking Marie to the side. "Why the hell didn't anyone invite me?"

"Mom, please lower your voice and stop swearing. I don't like Joseph to hear that kind of language," Beth said with disgust. Although Beth was used to Delilah's foul mouth – she heard it her entire life – she did not want her children exposed to such language.

"I don't give a shit what you like; I'll do as I damn well please," Delilah responded, posture erect, shoulders back, head held high.

"If you don't stop, Joseph and I will leave and you won't be able to spend time with him."

Marie interjected. "This is my house and you will do as I say or you will leave. I will not have yelling and swearing in my house."

Delilah shrugged her shoulders. "Humph. Since when did you become such a holy roller?"

"Since your mother and I invited Beth and Joseph."

Delilah's posture slumped. "Well, where's my coffee?"

Delilah sat quietly drinking her coffee while helping Margaret and Joseph with the puzzle. A few minutes later lunch was ready.

They all gathered and sat around the kitchen table, when Delilah noticed Beth wearing Margaret's locket.

"Isn't that Grandma's locket?"

"It was until Grandma gave it to me," Beth said with a smile, while glancing over at Margaret.

"Why should she give it to you?"

"Because I spent so much time with Grandma and Grandpa when I was young, and I helped them so much when I grew up. We developed a special bond."

"Oh, so you spent so much time with your grandmother when you were growing up, did you?"

"Yes, you were always busy doing something or other. Grandma, do you remember me sitting on your lap in front of the window, watching the traffic, teaching me the difference between a car and a truck and a bus? I loved those times."

"Yes, Beth, I do," Margaret said with a look of sheer joy.

Delilah sat up straight in her chair and squinted her eyes. "Oh, so now you think your grandmother raised you. Your grandmother didn't raise you, I raised you."

"All I'm saying, Mom, is that I spent a lot of time with Grandma and I have a lot of happy memories."

"And I didn't give you happy memories?"

"Mom now is not the time. Eat your lunch." Beth shook her head, lowered her eyes, and let out a sigh.

Oddly enough, Delilah did as Beth requested and everyone finished eating in peace.

Beth stood. "I'll help Aunt Marie clean up if you want to finish the puzzle with Joseph," Beth suggested.

"I'd love to," Margaret said, taking Joseph's hand and leading him into the other room. Delilah picked up her coffee cup and followed them. It wasn't long before Beth heard Joseph getting cranky.

Beth said, "He needs a nap."

"He can nap here," Marie offered.

"He doesn't have his Gizmo stuffed toy and he can't seem to sleep without it. I guess we all need some security."

"Don't worry about it, Beth. You take Joseph home. Grandma can help me finish."

"Okay, Aunt Marie, thank you."

Beth and Marie walked into the living room. "Grandma, Joseph and I are going to leave now. We'll be back later in the week. We'll come after lunch and we'll be sure to remember Gizmo."

Marie answered, "That would be nice. But don't come Thursday; Grandma has a doctor's appointment."

"Does Friday work?"

Before anyone could answer, Delilah stood up from her chair. "Why didn't anyone tell me my mother had a doctor's appointment? What time is her appointment? I'm going to go with."

"There is no need for you to come with. It's just my regular physical," Margaret said.

"I don't care. I'm going. What time is the appointment? If you don't tell me, I'll be sitting on the front stairs at seven a.m.," Delilah said with arms crossed on her chest.

Margaret, Marie, and Beth glanced at each other all shaking their heads in disbelief while raising their eyebrows towards Delilah.

"It's at eleven. We will leave here at ten thirty." With that, Marie let out a huge sigh.

Beth lifted Joseph into her arms. "Goodbye, Grandma. Goodbye, Mom. Goodbye, Aunt Marie and thank you."

"You're welcome, Beth. See you Friday."

א

When Beth arrived Friday, her Uncle Norman and his sister Bertha were also there.

"Hi, Uncle Norman and Aunt Bertha. I'm glad to see both of you here. Hi, Grandma," Beth said, then gave Margaret a peck on the check. Beth poked her head around the corner into the kitchen. "Hi, Aunt Marie."

"Hello, Beth."

Beth took a seat on the couch next to her grandmother. "How did your doctor's appointment go, Grandma?"

"My appointment went well, Beth. The doctor said my cancer is in remission. Isn't that wonderful! The only downside of the day was your mother. She keeps insisting that I come to live with her. You know that I don't want to. I just don't know what to do. I'm going to stay with Aunt Bertha for a few days to give Aunt Marie a little rest."

"Aunt Marie, can I put Joseph down for a nap?"

"Yes Beth, lay him down on my bed."

"Okay, thanks."

Beth laid Joseph down on her aunt's bed and tucked him in with Gizmo. As she bent down to kiss his cheek, he threw his arms around her neck, gave her a kiss on the cheek, and whispered, "I love you, Mommy sweetheart."

"I love you too, Joseph sweetheart. Have a good nap."

When Beth returned to the living room, she saw Delilah had arrived, uninvited. She was standing with her hands on her hips in front of Margaret.

"Ma, you need to come and live with me. I wrote down everything the doctor said yesterday, including all of the medications you're taking. I'll be able to provide better care than Bertha."

"It will only be for a few days, I'll be fine. Marie will give Bertha all of that information. In fact, I think we should give it to all of my children, then everyone will have it in case I need to stay somewhere else. The doctor doesn't have any concerns, and I just want to give Marie a break for a few days. Bertha will take good care of me."

"I should take care of you, not Bertha. You should come and stay with me," Delilah said defiantly.

"I've decided. I will stay with Bertha."

Norman spoke up. "I think it's a good idea for Mom to stay with Bertha, then Bertha will get used to caring for Mom in case she has to stay with her again."

"I agree," replied Bertha. "I need to get used to caring for Mom."

"Who cares what you need. Ma should be with me." Delilah's voice was forceful.

"We should all take turns so none of us becomes overburdened. I think that's what Mom wants too," Norman said.

"I don't give a shit what you think. Ma, don't you think you should live with me?"

Margaret began to tremble. "No, Delilah. I will stay at Bertha's house."

"Yes, Mom will stay with me."

Delilah clinched her fists and her face started to turn red. "How dare you side with Ma? You know she should stay with me."

"She's going to stay with me, Delilah, so just drop it."

Delilah walked into the kitchen where Marie was brewing a pot of coffee and took a steak knife from the drawer. She ran back into the living room to where Norman and Bertha were standing.

She lunged at Bertha. "You son-of-a-bitch."

Norman grabbed Delilah's arm so Delilah turned the knife on Norman.

Marie ran out of the kitchen and approached Delilah from behind, grabbing the knife, "You need to leave now."

Beth stood frozen in disbelief.

Delilah turned around, looking Marie in the eyes, while putting her hands on her hips. "I'll leave when I'm damn good and ready."

"Then you better be damn good and ready right now. Leave or I'm calling the police," Norman said.

Delilah headed towards the door. "I'll get even with all of you son-of-a-bitches."

Delilah slammed the door so hard that Joseph awoke from his nap.

Beth was horrified as she calmed Joseph down, lulling him back into sleep. She was glad he didn't witness his grandmother's rage. Although Beth was a victim of her mother's anger her whole life and had witnessed the abuse Delilah had waged on her grandma Helen and her father, somehow she was still surprised at the lengths she would go to get her way.

Chapter 10

Over the next six months, Margaret stayed with her daughter, Bertha, and her son, Brian, several weeks at a time, to give Marie a break. But Margaret was suffering the consequences. She telephoned Beth to let her know what was happening.

"Each time your mother finds out that I stayed with Uncle Brian or Aunt Bertha, she verbally abuses me, asking why I don't stay with her. Your mother says she is the one I should be living with. I tell her I'm taking turns. Though you know, Beth, except for your mother, Uncle Norman, Uncle Brian, and Aunt Bertha; my other children live far away. I try to give Marie a break. I don't want her to get sick."

"Don't worry, Grandma. You're doing the right thing," Beth said.

"Delilah doesn't care if Marie gets sick. She thinks I just stay with Bertha because Bertha doesn't like her. I told Delilah that I stay with my children because they are my children. Then she shouts that she is my child too. She says that Marie is not my child and I stay with her, and when I remind her that Norman is, she calls everyone dirty names and tells me to go to hell."

"I'm sorry, Grandma; I don't know what to tell you."

"I just don't know what to do anymore, Beth."

"I don't think there's anything anyone can do. My mother is who she is."

א

One autumn afternoon, Marie called Beth with some bad news.

"Grandma is in the hospital. She wasn't feeling well so I took her to the doctor. Her cancer is back. They are starting her back on chemo. They expect her to be in the hospital for about two weeks. She's asking for you. I hope you can visit her."

"Thanks for telling me. I'll go visit her tomorrow. What are they saying about her prognosis? Did you tell my mother?"

"The doctor believes that since they started chemo right away, her cancer will again go into remission. That's what we're all hoping for." There was a pause on the line before Marie continued. "I haven't called your mother yet. To be honest, I've been avoiding it. Your mother hasn't talked to anyone since Grandma has been staying with Uncle Brian and Aunt Bertha. She's mad at everyone because Grandma won't stay with her. Grandma won't stay with her because she's afraid. I can't force Grandma to stay with your mother. I don't want to talk to your mother. I think I'll ask Norman to call her tonight."

"I'll tell her if you'd like."

"No, I think Norman should be the one to tell her."

"Okay, if you think so. Do you have Grandma's phone number at the hospital? I'll call her this afternoon."

"Sure, she will be glad to hear from you."

Beth jotted down her grandma's telephone number on a scrap of paper. She dialed her grandmother's number then placed the scrap paper in her phonebook.

Margaret *was* glad Beth called. She was even happier to hear Beth would visit her the next day.

א

As Beth stepped off the hospital elevator the next afternoon, she heard a ruckus at the nurse's station. She turned to look.

It can't be.

She saw Delilah screaming at the nurse. She walked towards Margaret's room as quickly as she could; hoping Delilah would not see her. She pushed open Margaret's door.

"Hi Grandma, how are you feeling?"

Margaret was shaking. "Better, now that you are here. Beth, sweetheart, your mother was here. I don't know where she went, but she was very mad."

"Grandma, calm down. Don't worry about my mother." Beth was shaking her head.

"But Beth, she started to scream at me. She asked why I didn't call her to bring me to the hospital. She told me the only reason I'm sick is because I'm living with Norman and Marie. She doesn't think they take good care of me."

"Grandma, Aunt Marie takes very good care of you. Your cancer has nothing to do with where you live or who you live with."

"But Beth, she has gotten me so upset. I don't like all that yelling."

"I know, Grandma. I brought my beautiful smile," Beth said, trying to think of anything that would calm her grandmother down.

Margaret sighed. "Thanks Beth, you're right. I shouldn't let her upset me."

"All you need to worry about now is getting better."

"I know."

Just then the door flung open. Delilah thrust herself through the open door.

"Those son-of-a-bitches. They won't tell me anything. They said that Norman and Marie are the only ones with power of attorney. They are the only ones the nurses are allowed to talk to. I'm her daughter. I should know what's going on."

Margaret began to cry. "Please Delilah, please stop."

"This is all your fault. You're the one that gave Norman and Marie this power. Now you can live with the ramifications of your decisions or die by them. Don't ask me to help you if I don't know what's going on."

Beth felt so bad for her Grandma. "Mom, please stop. Grandma won't get better if she's upset. She needs peace and quiet."

"I don't care what that bitch needs. This is all her fault." Delilah was pacing back and forth across the room.

Margaret began to cry harder. "Delilah, please stop."

Beth pushed the nurse's call button. Two nurses entered the room. "What do you need Margaret? Why are you crying?"

"She needs to go to hell," Delilah said "I'm her daughter; I need to know what's going on."

One of the nurses left the room, while the other tried to calm Margaret. "Maybe you should both go into the hall."

"I'm not going anywhere. I'm staying right here," Delilah said as she arched her back.

"Please, Mom, let's wait in the hall until Grandma gets calmed down."

"I'm not going anywhere."

The second nurse returned with the security guard.

"Come on, ma'am, let's go outside."

"I'm not going anywhere."

The security officer reached for Delilah's elbow. "Come on, ma'am."

Delilah jerked away. "Keep your filthy hands off me, you son-of-a-bitch. Don't touch me."

"Mom, stop. Let's go outside."

Margaret began to cry so hard she couldn't breathe.

"Mom, please."

"Leave now, ma'am or I'll have you arrested for disorderly conduct."

"Mom, you don't want to go to jail. Let's leave."

"Fine." Delilah turned to Margaret. "Goodbye, bitch."

The security guard escorted both Beth and Delilah out the front door.

"Okay, Mom, go right home. I'll call you tonight. I have to use the bathroom."

"Are you going back up to see that bitch?"

"I don't know. I'll call you tonight."

Beth walked back into the hospital lobby and found the nearest bathroom. She was so upset with her mother's antics that she threw up.

Beth went back to visit Margaret. A security guard

was standing in the corner of Margaret's room, legs spread apart, hands behind his back. A nurse was taking Margaret's vital signs. As Beth started to enter the room, the guard took a step forward. Margaret turned her head towards the door, her voice shaky. "It's okay. This is my granddaughter Beth."

The guard stepped back. The nurse said, "Margaret's blood pressure is elevated, and we're concerned she might have a stroke."

Beth sat down on Margaret's bed and took her hand, which was cold and clammy. "Grandma, calm down. I know my mother upset you but she's gone. She won't be back today."

"Beth, I don't want her here at all anymore." Margaret was trembling. "Every time I see her or talk to her, she upsets me. How can we keep her away? She scares me."

The nurse responded, "While you are here, your door will remain closed. We will have a note on the door directing everyone to come to the nurse's station for permission to enter your room. With your help, we can create a list of who can enter and, of course, who cannot. Your daughter will be denied access."

Margaret was still trembling. "Do you really think that will stop her? What do you think, Beth?"

Before Beth could respond, the nurse answered, "If she enters your room, security will have her arrested."

Beth tilted her head. "Can we have security outside the door around the clock?"

"You know ma'am, that's a great idea," the guard said. "The situation would be defused before it could escalate."

"Yes and my grandma wouldn't have to deal with my mother and get upset. That can't happen again. We don't want Grandma having a stroke."

Margaret squeezed Beth's hand while letting out a sigh of relief. "Thank you, Beth."

"You're welcome, Grandma. You know I will do anything to help you." Beth looked at the guard. "How soon can we make this happen?"

"I'll get on it right away. I will be here until three; however, I can stay later if they need me to. Let me go talk to my manager. We'll make this happen."

Beth got up from the bed, walked over to the guard, and shook his hand. "Thank you."

"This helps us too. Your mother caused quite a commotion in the hallway earlier today. Several of the patients were upset, as were the nurses. Keeping your mother away will help everyone." The guard walked toward the door. "Let me see what I can do."

The nurse finished her assessment. "Margaret, I'm going to go now. You try to relax. Here's your call button. Call me if you need anything."

"Thank you, nurse, I will."

As the nurse turned to leave, Beth asked, "Can we have my mother banned from calling too?"

"That's a great idea. I'll call the switchboard when I get back to the nurse's station. Thanks for the suggestion and for your help."

"I just want what's best for Grandma." Beth glanced at Margaret and they exchanged smiles.

The nurse left and closed the door behind her. Beth pulled a chair up to Margaret's bed and sat down. "Do you feel better now, Grandma?"

"Yes, Beth, I do. Thank you for all your help. I don't know what I would have done today without you here."

"No thanks needed. I'll always help you." Beth got up and kissed her grandma's forehead. "I'm going to leave now. The nurses and security will make sure you are safe. Get some rest, you need it. I'll call you after dinner."

As Beth stood smiling at her grandmother, she noticed Margaret's body beginning to relax.

ש

Beth called Margaret after dinner.

"Hi, Grandma. Did you rest? Are you feeling better?"

Beth heard a lilt in Margaret's voice. "They kept their promise. There has been someone outside my door since you left. I feel so much better. Now I won't have to worry about your mother. Thank you so much, sweetheart."

"You're welcome, Grandma. Just so you know, we established a password so my mother can't call and pretend to be me or someone else you know. I'll call Uncle Norman, Aunt Bertha, and Uncle Brian with the password. Is there anyone else you would like me to call?"

"No, I can't imagine who else would call."

"The operator will take the name and phone number of anyone who doesn't know the password. You can decide who you would like to call back."

"That's a wonderful idea, Beth. I'm so relieved."

"I'm glad. You have a good night sleep. I'll call you tomorrow. Goodnight Grandma."

"Goodnight, sweetheart. Thank you."

Beth called her Uncle Norman, Aunt Bertha, and Uncle Brian. She told them about the password. "Grandma does not want my mother to phone or visit. Please don't give her the password." They all heartily agreed.

Next she had to tell Delilah. She bit her lip and dialed her mother's number.

"Mom, Grandma doesn't want you to phone or visit. A security guard is posted outside Grandma's door. Someone will be posted twenty-four hours a day. They will not allow you into Grandma's room, so if you show up, they will have you arrested. And if you try and call, they won't put your phone calls through. The nurses won't discuss Grandma's care with you, so don't even bother trying. I suggest you stay away and don't try to call."

Beth heard rage in her mother's voice. "All those

son-of-a-bitches can go to hell. Your asshole grandmother can drop dead for all I care. All she cares about anyway is her precious Norman. He can go to hell too."

"Mom, I hear that you're upset. I'll let you go."

As Beth was hanging up, she heard Delilah still screaming into the phone.

Three days after Margaret's encounter with Delilah, she was released from the hospital. After Margaret was settled, she called Beth.

"Hi Beth, I'm back at Uncle Norman's. He picked me up from the hospital this morning. I'm glad I haven't seen or heard from your mother. It has been so peaceful without her."

"I'm glad you're home. Joseph and I will visit you on Wednesday, if you're up to it. Have Aunt Marie call me to make sure it's okay. You rest now."

א

Beth began to visit her grandmother weekly and phoned her almost every day. Margaret continued to give Marie a break and stay with her other children for a few days every so often. Everyone was relieved that there had been no interaction with Delilah, that was until Marie became extremely ill.

Margaret called Beth. "Aunt Marie is sick. I have to live somewhere else until she recovers. My only option is your mother. Aunt Bertha's children are sick and Uncle

Brian is out of town. I called my other children but no one else can come to town for a few days and help me." Beth could hear the tension in Margaret's voice. "Beth, can I stay with you? I'm afraid to live with your mother."

"Yes Grandma, you can. I can pick you up after Joseph wakes from his nap."

"Thank you, Beth. Do you have to ask Edward?"

"Yes, I'll talk to Edward, but I'm sure he'll say it's okay. I'll call him at work right now, and then I'll call you back."

Beth called Edward at work. "Hi honey. My Aunt Marie is sick, so grandma called to ask if she can stay with us until Aunt Marie feels better. Nobody, except possibly my mother, is available, and no one, including Grandma, wants her to live with my mother."

"Of course your grandma can stay with us. When will you bring her home? Do you need me to come home early?"

"No, I'll pick her up as soon as Joseph wakes from his nap. I'll call Aunt Marie to make sure Grandma is ready. I should be home before the boys get home from school. Thank you for letting Grandma stay."

"You're welcome. I love your grandma too. She's always welcome."

"I'll see you when you get home. I love you."

Beth was excited to call Margaret. "Edward said it is fine for you to stay with us. I'm going to enjoy having you with me."

Margaret began to cry. "Marie didn't know I talked to you. She called your mother. Your mother is here now packing me up. I don't want to go. I'm afraid she will treat me the way she treated your grandma Helen. Oh Beth, I don't want to die. I'm afraid I'll die if I live with your mother, just like your grandma Helen did."

Beth's lip began to twitch. "Grandma, don't even think that."

"It could happen. What can we do?"

"Call my mother to the phone, maybe I can talk to her."

Margaret returned, still crying. "She won't come to the phone. She said she is taking me with her; she doesn't care what anybody says. She also said you are not on her call list."

"Grandma, I'm so sorry. I wish Aunt Marie hadn't called her."

"Me too."

Delilah grabbed the phone. "She has to go now."

Beth heard the phone slam.

Beth sat at her kitchen table, cradled her head in her hands, and began to cry. "Please God, keep her safe."

Joseph walked into the kitchen with a book in his hand, rubbing his eyes from sleep. Beth hastily wiped the tears from her eyes.

"Read a book?" he said, holding the book out to his mother.

"Sure, sweetheart," she said and pulled the small boy onto her lap.

Reading would help keep her mind off Margaret for a little while. She also had Joseph help her bake a cake for dessert.

When Beth's other two sons, Jon and Jack, returned from school, they ran through the front door. "Yum, what smells so good?"

"Joseph made dessert."

"Thanks, Joseph!" they said in unison.

The boys ran into the kitchen for their snacks.

Edward came home early. He walked up the stairs and into the kitchen where Beth was cooking dinner.

"I know you told me not to but I had to come home early. I'm excited that your grandma will be with us."

"She won't be with us." Beth began to cry.

"Why not?"

"My mother found out." Edward gasped as Beth continued. "My mother refused to let Grandma stay with us. She took her home. Grandma is so scared. She didn't want to go."

"I know, Beth, I know. Let's just hope she'll be okay."

Edward held Beth in his arms while she cried. "Let's just hope."

Chapter 11

Three days later, Delilah called Beth.

"I have an appointment with Doctor Cube. This son-of-a-bitch has me so upset. All she does is ask me if I've called Marie or if Marie is feeling better. She keeps insisting on going back to live with Norman. I can't take her anymore. I'm sick of hearing about Norman and Marie."

"Hopefully Aunt Marie will be feeling better soon, then Grandma can move back with them. In the meantime, she can stay with me."

"She will never move back with Norman, I'll make sure of that, but you can have her today if you want. Without her tagging along, I'll be able to talk to Doctor Cube privately."

Beth was conflicted. Of course she wanted Margaret with her. She felt she would be taking Margaret out of harm's way temporarily, especially since Delilah was starting to say the same things about Margaret that she had said about Helen. But Beth did not want to enable the relationship she believed was occurring between Delilah and Doctor Cube, which she didn't think was right, besides that fact that it would feel as if she were betraying her father, as well. She recalled the meeting that occurred several years ago in the restaurant parking lot between her mother and Doctor Cube.

I can't take this anymore. Beth thought to herself. *What should I do?* She finally decided that keeping Margaret safe was a priority. Beth knew that Delilah was going to do whatever she wanted without a second thought about anyone, whether Beth enabled her or not. She also believed that if she were to explain her decision to Mike, he would understand.

"Of course, Grandma can spend the day with me. In fact, she can spend several days."

"That won't be necessary. I'm sure I'll feel better after seeing Doctor Cube. We'll be there soon."

An hour later Delilah and Margaret appeared at Beth's door. Beth was surprised to see Margaret with a black eye.

"Oh my gosh, Grandma, what happened?"

"Clumsy me, I tripped and hit my head on the china cabinet," Margaret answered while looking out of the corner of her eye at Delilah.

"Yeah," Delilah answered with a smirk, "how clumsy."

Margaret and Beth walked upstairs into the living room. "Let me take your jacket, Grandma."

Margaret took off her jacket and handed it to Beth. "I love spring. It's my favorite time of the year."

"I love spring too," Beth said as she hung Margaret's jacket in the closet. "Make yourself comfortable."

"Well, isn't that cozy; everyone in love," Delilah said snidely. "I don't know when I'll be back. It depends how long my doctor visit takes." Then she walked out the door, pulling it closed behind her.

Margaret sat down on the sofa.

"I'll bring you a cup of coffee, Grandma, then we'll talk." Beth turned and went into the kitchen. A few minutes later she returned to the living room carrying two cups of coffee and a plate of warm cookies. "I made these cookies just for you. I know oatmeal-raisin are your favorite."

"Yes they are. I smelled them when I came in and hoped we would have some."

Margaret took a cookie from the plate and took a sip of coffee.

"Okay Grandma, fess up. How did you get that black eye?"

Tears started to fall down Margaret's cheeks. She put her coffee and cookie down on the coffee table. "Beth,

I'm so scared. I want to live with Uncle Norman. Can you call Aunt Marie? Your mother refuses to call her."

"I'll call Aunt Marie, but first, how did you get that black eye?"

Margaret rolled up the arms of her sweater. Both arms were bruised.

Beth gasped. "Oh my gosh, Grandma."

"I asked your mother to call Aunt Marie to find out how she was feeling. Your mother refused. She said, 'Marie can go to hell.' I told her I wanted to go back to Uncle Norman's. She grabbed my arms and started to shake me. I hit my head on the china cabinet. As she was shaking me, she screamed at me saying I'll never go back to Norman."

"Grandma, I'm so sorry. What do you want me to do? Should I call the police?"

"No, if you do anything, she'll get mad at me for telling you."

"Yeah, then you'll get beat and punished. She did the same thing to me throughout my childhood. I understand what you're going through. Maybe we should tell Uncle Norman. Maybe there is something he can do."

"Please try to call Aunt Marie," Margaret said with urgency.

"Let's go call."

Margaret and Beth walked to the kitchen. Beth dialed Aunt Marie's number and handed the phone to Margaret. "Hi Marie, are you feeling any better? I'm at Beth's. Delilah had an appointment. When can I come back?"

Margaret listened for a few minutes, then replied. "Okay, feel better. Here's Beth."

Margaret handed Beth the phone. "Hi Aunt Marie. Are you feeling better?"

"I'm feeling better," Aunt Marie replied, "but it will probably be a few more days."

"Aunt Marie, I have to tell you something, but you can't let my mother know." Beth relayed the story Margaret had told her.

"Is Grandma okay?" Marie asked with terror in her voice.

"She appears to be, except for the bruises, and the fact that she is scared to death. Do you think there's anything Uncle Norman can do?"

"I don't know. I'll talk to him as soon as he gets home. Maybe we can have someone stay here during the day until I feel better. I'm so sorry I got sick. I feel so bad for Grandma."

"You can't help that you got sick. Talk to Uncle Norman and see what he thinks."

"What time will your mother be back?"

"I don't know. She went to see Doctor Cube."

"Oh, that may take some time," Marie said sarcastically. "I've listened to your mother's stories about Doctor Cube."

"Well, I want to spend time with Grandma, so I'll talk to you later. Bye."

"Bye, Beth. Thanks for calling."

Margaret and Beth spent the rest of the afternoon recalling happier times. Margaret shared the time when she was five years old, leaning against the iron fence in front of the school on her block.

"Wouldn't you know, that damned bustle got caught between the iron posts." Margaret's face turned red with embarrassment and laughter.

Beth added, "Remember when grandpa would walk to the corner grocery store every day after dinner? By the time you and I had the dishes washed and put away, he would be back with one Pepsi we all shared in an ice cream cup for each of us."

"I loved having you with us. I miss Grandpa."

"I do too."

The doorbell rang, and Margaret's face turned white. "I hope that's not your mother. I don't want to go back with her. I'm scared."

Beth walked down the stairs and unlocked the door. Delilah pushed the door open, standing tall and straight, pushing out her flat chest. "How has the son-of-a-bitch been?"

"If you mean Grandma, she's been wonderful."

"Yeah, that's the son-of-a-bitch I mean. How can anything be wonderful with her?"

"It has been. Please don't swear in my house."

"I'll swear any damn place I feel like swearing."

"Well don't do it here." Beth took a deep breath. "How was your appointment?"

"Don't worry about it," Delilah said with disdain.

They walked up the stairs and into the kitchen where Margaret was sitting.

"Let's go. Get your jacket," Delilah ordered. "Mike likes dinner ready when he gets home."

Margaret's voice was trembling. "Delilah, can you take me to Norman's?"

Delilah flew into a rage, flailing her arms in the air, stamping her feet on the floor, and screaming at the top of her lungs.

"I told you, you son-of-a-bitch, you'll never go back to that asshole."

Margaret put her head down and raised her tearful eyes at Beth. Beth's heart broke for her Grandma, but there was nothing she could do. *I sure hope Uncle Norman can help*, she thought.

Beth walked to the closet and got Margaret's jacket. "Your grandma thanks you for the wonderful day. I hope we can do it again soon," Delilah said with a smirk and yanked the jacket out of Beth's hand.

With sadness in her voice, Margaret said goodbye to Beth. Beth hugged her grandma goodbye and gave her a kiss on the cheek.

Delilah was already at the bottom of the stairs. "Come on, let's go. Cut the crap."

Margaret and Beth looked at each other, sadness

on both of their faces. Beth stood at the top of the stairs watching Margaret descend and walk out the door with Delilah. She walked down the stairs, closed and locked the door. She walked back upstairs into the living room and to the large picture window where she stood watching Delilah back her car out of the driveway. She began to weep. Beth sat on the sofa, sad and dazed as she thought to herself, *Why is my mother like that? Why is she so hateful? She only seems happy when she's making other people sad. I don't understand.*

About an hour after she left, Delilah called Beth to complain.

"All this son-of-a-bitch did on the way home was say she wanted to go to Norman's. She begged me to take her. I'll be damned if she'll ever go back there. She's shunning me and neglecting my feelings. She only cares about Norman."

"They have always been close."

"But I'm the baby. She should want to be with me," she said in a damaged tone.

"Try to be a little more patient and gentle. I'm sure Grandma sometimes does not admit that she's not feeling well. Cancer does strange things."

"What about her being patient and gentle with me. What about her not always saying she wants to go to Norman. She'll never go back to Norman."

"Mom, I'm just saying, maybe if you were nicer, she would be nicer," Beth replied.

"I better go. The son-of-a-bitch is coming out of the bathroom."

Before Beth could answer, Delilah hung up.

Later that evening, after Beth, Edward, and their three sons finished dinner, Beth called her Uncle Norman. "Hi, Uncle Norman. Did Aunt Marie tell you I called?"

"Yeah, she did. So what's up? Your mother has been pushing Grandma?"

"It's terrible. Grandma is so scared. I'm so scared. I keep remembering the horrible things my mother did to my grandma Helen. Is there anything you can do?"

"I'll call my friend Rick Casey. He's a detective with the Chicago PD. I'll call your mother and tell her I'll pick Grandma up tomorrow after work. I'll get someone to stay here until Aunt Marie feels better. How does that sound?"

"That'll be great if it works. My mother said she will never let Grandma go back to you. I'm afraid of what she'll do."

"I don't know what else I can do, Beth. If you come up with another idea, let me know, but for now, that's the plan."

"That's better than nothing. Let me know if I can help."

꙼

The following afternoon, Delilah telephoned Beth.

"I took your grandmother to Doctor Cube this morning for a checkup. He said that although the son-of-a-bitch has cancer, it appears to be in remission. He said she was otherwise healthy and should live many more years. That's not what I wanted to hear."

"Mom, don't say that."

"Well it's true. If she were dead, I wouldn't have to listen to her beg to go to Norman's."

"If you let her go back to Uncle Norman, you wouldn't have to listen to her," Beth said, trying to reason with her.

"She'll never go back. He called last night. He thinks he's picking her up today. He doesn't know I'm taking her to Johnston. We're leaving as soon as your father gets home."

Beth swallowed a lump in her throat, frightened by what she had just heard. "Mom, if you let her live with Uncle Norman, she won't keep stressing you out."

"She'll never live with him. I gotta go, your father is here."

Beth stood frozen, then she began to panic. She tried to call her Aunt Marie but there was no answer. She didn't know what to do. About thirty minutes later Uncle Norman called.

"Beth, I'm at a payphone down the street from your mother's house. No one is home. Do you know where Grandma is?"

"Yes. She's on her way to Johnston."

"What the hell. I can't believe your mother did that. She's rotten to the core."

"I know. I'm afraid there is nothing we can do," Beth said through sniffles. "I'm so scared for Grandma."

"Me too, Beth, me too."

Chapter 12

The following afternoon, Beth received a phone call from her Aunt Louise.

"We're in Johnston. Joey has a few days off work, and he decided he wanted to come to Johnston to fish and visit family. While we were in town, Joey noticed your father at the gas station. Boy, they were both surprised. Beth, did you know they were here?"

"Yeah, I found out yesterday."

"Do you know your grandmother is with them?"

"Yes, and I'm not happy about it."

Louise's voice began to tremble. "Your dad invited us to their house," she took a large gasp of air. "It broke my heart. Your grandmother had numerous bruises on her arms, legs, and face."

"Oh my gosh. Did you ask about them?"

"Your mother said they were the result of the cancer, but when she said that, your grandma shook her head."

Beth's mouth dropped open. She had to sit down. "Did you talk to Grandma?"

"No, we didn't have time alone." Beth heard a chime. "I don't have much time left on this payphone but I want to tell you, your grandma's bruises were deep purple and looked like blood blisters rather than regular bruises. I've got to go now, but I'll call you from the hotel tonight."

"Okay, thanks for telling me. Try and talk to Grandma if you can."

"I will."

Beth heard from Louise that evening.

"I was able to talk to your grandmother when your dad and Joey went outside and your mother went to the bathroom. When I asked your grandma what happened, she began to cry. She said your mother hits her, grabs her, and shakes her. She asked me not to say anything because she's afraid of your mother finding out, causing her to abuse her more. Beth, how can I help you, what can I do?"

"How much longer will you be in Johnston? It would help if you can spend as much time as you can with my grandmother. I don't think my mother will abuse her with you there. Continue to observe and try to talk to Grandma. I'll call the social worker in the morning. Maybe she can offer some advice."

"Unfortunately, we'll be here just one more day. Joey wants to spend his birthday here, near his parents, and then he wants to leave. I'll stay with your grandma as much as I can," Louise said with a sigh, "but your mother will slap her whether I'm there or not."

"What do you mean?"

Louise hesitated. "When we returned to your parents' house this afternoon, after I called you, your grandma was walking toward her bedroom. Your mother was walking behind her. Your grandmother stopped and asked your mother to please let her go back to your uncle Norman's. Your mother became enraged. She hit your grandma so hard she fell into the couch, complaining that her hip hurt. Your mother told your grandmother she will never return to Norman and she didn't care if her hip hurt."

Beth began to cry. "I don't know how to help my grandma. Uncle Norman and Aunt Marie helped block my mother, but now that she has taken Grandma to Johnston, they can't help."

"I am so sorry, Beth. I will spend as much time with your grandma as I can. I'll call you tomorrow."

"Thanks, Louise."

After a sleepless night, Beth managed to get Edward and the children ready for their day. After Edward and their two sons left, Beth sat Joseph in front of the television with some toys and books.

"Mommy has to make a phone call. Watch Sesame

114

Street and play with your toys. I'll be back as soon as I can."

"Okay Mommy," Joseph said. He pointed to the television. "Look, Big Bird."

"Yay, Big Bird."

Joseph clapped his hands. "Yay!"

Beth went to the kitchen, sat on a chair, and grabbed the phone. She took a deep breath, then dialed.

"I'd like to speak to Sandy Ramey, please."

"Sandy is no longer with the agency, can I give you to someone else?"

"Shoot. Yes please, I would like to speak to someone."

"What is your name?"

"Bethany Jasdam."

"Okay, let me see who's available."

"Thank you."

Beth sat in frustration. *Now I'll have to relay the entire story again.*

"Hello, this is Linda Bracken, how can I help you?"

"This is Bethany Jasdam. I've called before."

"Yes, Bethany, I see you've called before," she replied sarcastically.

Beth relayed the story her Aunt Louise told her.

"Since your grandmother is out of our jurisdiction, there is nothing we can do," Linda said "You'll have to call social services in Johnston."

"Thank you." Beth hung up the phone, *for nothing.*

Beth went to read Joseph a book. She thought she

would research the phone number for Johnston social services after lunch, when Joseph was taking his nap. She never got the chance.

She just laid Joseph down and was walking back to the kitchen to get her Johnston phone book, when the telephone rang. As she answered, she heard sobs.

"Beth, I have some terrible news. When Joey and I got to your parents' house this morning, your grandma was already up, washed, and dressed. Your mother had her in the bathroom and was yelling at her to take her pills. Your grandma was crying really hard. I felt so bad. As they came out of the bathroom, your mother was dragging your grandma. Your grandma could not walk. Delilah sat your grandma on a kitchen chair, but she couldn't sit up straight. I didn't want her to fall off the chair so I moved another chair next to her and sat down so I could put my arm around her and hold her up."

"Maybe I should get on a plane and get out there."

"Wait, Beth, let me finish."

Beth sensed urgency in Louise's voice, even through her sobs.

"As I was holding your grandmother, your mother came over and pinched your grandma's cheeks together to open her mouth. She stuffed several pills into your grandma's mouth and squeezed your grandma's nose so she would swallow. I tried to stop her but she pushed me away. She twisted my shoulder so hard, I was afraid to try again. Joey and your dad walked over, but she pushed both of them away too. Then she grabbed your grandma's wrists and started to drag her towards the bedroom. Your dad and Joey lifted your grandma, carried her to her bedroom, and laid her in bed. Your mother began to pound your father. He raised his arms to block her punches but she pushed him over."

Beth sat hard in a chair and put her hand over her mouth in disbelief.

"She barged past him and grabbed your grandma under her arms, dragging her out of bed toward the kitchen. Your grandma was so groggy, she didn't even cry. Your mother dragged your grandma to the kitchen sink, stood behind her to support her, and threw cold water in your grandma's face. While the water was hitting your grandma's face, she took her last breath. Beth, I'm so sorry, your grandmother is gone."

Beth froze in shock and disbelief, then began to cry. "No, it can't be true. Doctor Cube said Grandma was healthy. How can she be gone?"

"I'm sorry, Beth. Your mother checked for a pulse, then started to laugh. Your grandma started to slide down so your father, Joey, and I ran to grab her while your mother continued to laugh. We lifted your grandma's lifeless body and carried her to bed. Your mother followed us and began to undress her. We all left the room. I was shocked at the scene that was unfolding before me, but I didn't want to stand around to watch your mother expose your grandmother's body; I wanted to at least show your grandmother that dignity. Your mother washed your grandmother and changed her clothes while we all sat in the kitchen wondering what we should do.

"When your mother was finished, she asked us to help put your grandmother in the van. Your mother grabbed Margaret under her arms and started dragging her out the door. Your father, Joey, and I lifted your grandma, breaking your mother's hold, and carried her to the van. Your mother got into the van, grabbed your grandmother under her arms again, and started pulling her into the van. Your grandma's arms and legs were twisting and getting caught on the door and seatbelt as your mother pulled, trying to get her in. Joey and I stepped into the van and told your mother we would help, so your mother eventually let go. Joey and I lifted your grandmother and laid her on the back seat, then we came back to the hotel to call you."

"Where did they take her?"

"To the hospital in Forest Springs."

"Why did they take her there?"

"I don't know, Beth. I'm just shocked by the whole incident."

"Thanks for calling," Beth answered, still in a state of disbelief.

After she hung up the phone, Beth folded her arms on the table, laid her head on top of her arms and cried uncontrollably. When she cried herself out, she raised her head and glanced out the window. *Poor Uncle Norman.*

Now Grandma will never return to him. She laid her head back down and cried some more.

The telephone rang. Beth sniffled and wiped her cheeks with the sleeve of her sweater.

"Yahoo, the son-of-a-bitch is dead! Now let's see her go back to her precious Norman."

"I can't believe it, Grandma is gone. Just two weeks ago Grandma was asking to stay with me, now she's gone."

"Well, believe it. Water's Funeral Home will drive her back to Chicago. I'll meet with the funeral director there tomorrow."

"I heard you took Grandma to the hospital."

"Yeah I did. That was a mistake."

"Why?'

"Well, your father pulled up to the door and I went into the emergency room. I told the receptionist I needed help with my mother, who I believed was dying. They ran outside with the gurney and loaded the son-of-a-bitch on, then wheeled her inside. They lifted her onto a bed and the doctor came right over. He examined her and pronounced her dead on arrival. He said the cause of death was heart failure, then said it appeared that she had been dead for several hours and asked why it took so long for me to try to get her help. He asked why I didn't call the EMS or take her to the clinic in Johnston, which would have been a lot closer than Forest Springs."

"So, why didn't you call EMS or take Grandma to the clinic in Johnston?"

"She was already dead; what could they do?" Delilah answered with a smirk.

"They may have been able to revive her."

"No, I don't think so," Delilah said sarcastically. "That asshole doctor sounded very accusatory. When I told him I washed her and changed her clothes before bringing her, he said people only do that when they have something to hide. Then he asked me what I was hiding and he questioned me about Grandma's bruises. I told them they must have gotten there when I tried getting her into the van all by myself, but he knew they were old bruises. I told him I took good care of your grandmother."

Beth was shaking. "I can't talk to you now, Mom. Call me when you make funeral arrangements."

Beth hung up the phone, laid her arms and head back on the kitchen table, and again, began to cry.

Chapter 13

The following afternoon, Beth was going through the motions of life as normal, though her heart was broken. Amidst her daily chores came bursts of tears. She felt the urge to call her grandmother, only to be brought back to the realization that Margaret was gone. Beth was still in a state of shock.

She wasn't prepared to have a conversation with Delilah when she called.

"I'm so mad. By the time I got to the funeral home, all the arrangements were already made. Nobody told me that asshole Brian brought Grandma to the funeral home several months ago. She gave the funeral director her clothes and picked out her coffin. She even picked out the songs and flowers she wanted. There was nothing for me to do. They can all go to hell."

"Well, Mom, at least you didn't have to deal with the stress of making all the arrangements."

"I should have made all the arrangements. I'm the baby."

"So when is the wake and funeral?" Beth asked, unable to continue to listen to her mother's rants.

"The wake is tomorrow. The funeral will be the next day. Did you know that Brian also took Grandma to the restaurant she wanted for the funeral lunch? That has been arranged too."

"How thoughtful of Grandma. What time is the wake and funeral?"

"I was so mad I forgot to ask."

Beth was so disgusted with her mother, she didn't want to talk to her any longer. "I'll call the funeral home for times. I need to call Edward so he can get the time off of work and get the boys out of school. I have to go. I'll see you at the wake."

"If I show up. I'm so mad, I may not go."

"That's your choice. I have to go. Goodbye."

Beth hung up the phone more heartbroken than ever. She was shocked that Delilah showed no remorse, no sadness at her own mother's passing. She felt Delilah's only concern was that no one was paying attention to her now that Grandma was dead and that she was unable to control the funeral or the luncheon afterwards.

When Beth and Edward arrived at the wake the following day, her Uncle Norman approached her and gave her a long, hard hug.

"Hi sweetheart, I'm glad you're here. Grandma loved you so much."

"She loved you too."

Beth saw sadness in her uncle's eyes, the same beautiful blue-gray eyes of her grandmother. As he wiped a tear from those beautiful eyes, he replied, "I wish we could have saved her."

"I know, Unc, I wish we could have too."

Beth's Aunt Marie approached, her eyes red and swollen from crying. She gave Beth another long hug. "I wish I hadn't gotten sick. I wish I knew Grandma had called you, then I wouldn't have called your mother and Grandma might still be alive."

Beth could no longer control her emotions, and tears began to stream down her cheeks. "If only...None of that matters now. All that matters is that Grandma will no longer be in pain. I'm sure it would have gotten worse as her cancer progressed," Beth said, trying to convince herself. "And she won't have to put up with my mother anymore."

She noticed tears in her uncle's eyes. "That's the only good thing," Norman responded.

Beth glanced at the front of the room. She saw her mother standing with some cousins, laughing. She gave her aunt and uncle another hug, then began to walk towards her mother. As she approached, she heard her mother, through laughter. "She won't go back to Norman now, will she?"

When Delilah saw Beth, she stopped laughing and took a step back. "Oh Beth, what am I going to do without Grandma?" Beth noticed a slight grin on her mother's face.

The cousins shook their heads and walked away. Delilah's hypocrisy nauseated Beth. "I don't know, Mom."

"Look at these beautiful flowers I bought," Delilah said, motioning to the arrangement next to the casket. "I'm the only one that bought flowers on my own."

"They're beautiful, Mom." Beth turned toward Margaret's casket. "I need to spend time with Grandma."

Beth approached the casket and noticed that her grandmother had on the dress she wore to Beth's wedding just ten years earlier. She knelt to pray as uncontrollable tears fell from her cheeks and onto her chest. Edward stood behind her and put his hand on her shoulder. She stood up, turned toward Edward, laid her head on his chest, and cried, his strong arms embracing her. Uncle Brian approached, putting his hand on Beth's back. Beth turned to him.

"Beth, Grandma wanted you to know, she chose that dress because your wedding day was the happiest day of her life. She loved you."

Beth hugged her Uncle Brian. "Thanks, Uncle Brian, that means a lot to me."

Edward stayed at Beth's side with his arm around her waist.

Beth glanced out of the corner of her eye to see

Delilah standing a few feet away, her upper lip tucked under her lower lip, with her cheeks flaring in and out. Beth turned to look straight at her. Delilah's brow furrowed, her eyes squinted, and she turned and walked away.

Delilah went to sit on the sofa directly across from the front door. This gave her a vantage point to be the first to communicate with anyone coming to pay respects. One of Margaret's brothers walked through the door. Delilah jumped up and ran to him.

"Oh, Uncle Richard, what am I going to do without my mother? We were so close. I can't imagine my life without her. I was always her favorite you know." Delilah laid her head on her uncle's shoulder as she gave him a hug. As Beth watched, she saw a sneer spread across Delilah's face.

Beth grew weary of her mother's antics. She took a seat at the back of the chapel, keeping her grandmother in her line of vision. Edward sat next to her. Beth laid her head on his shoulder as she wondered what more she could have done to save her grandmother's life.

The funeral was the following day. It was held in the funeral home chapel following Margaret's request. Delilah sat next to Beth, Edward, and their three sons. Edward held Joseph on his lap.

"Why is Mommy crying?" Joseph asked.

"Because her Grandma went to heaven, and she is sad."

Joseph gasped, "With Jesus?"

"Yes, with Jesus."

"That should make Mommy happy."

"It should, but Mommy is still sad."

Joseph bent over and kissed Beth's cheek. "Don't be sad, Mommy."

"Thank you, sweetheart," Beth said as tears streamed down her cheeks. "You make Mommy feel better."

"Good."

"Humph. I wish my kid would make me feel better," Delilah said in a petulant tone.

"Mom, I can't do this now."

As family and friends began to enter the chapel, Delilah rose and went to greet them. She had an air of superiority, stepping in front of her siblings when someone approached them. Beth sat watching, wishing this was all a bad dream that she would soon wake up from. Beth's Uncle Joey and Aunt Louise entered, first greeting Mike, who was standing at the back of the chapel.

Beth heard her father. "Hi, Joe. Thanks for your help in Johnston. I can't believe what happened. It was like a nightmare. Louise, thank you too. Thanks for comforting Beth. She was so close to Margaret."

"You're welcome," Louise said as she gave Mike a hug. "I'm glad we were there."

Mike stood slumped, head down. "Me too."

Louise put her arms out to Beth. Beth stood and walked to her aunt. Together they hugged and cried.

"I'm so sorry, Beth."

Beth could not speak. Joey outstretched his hand to Edward, as Edward stood. They shook hands, both looking at Beth with sorrow in their eyes.

Delilah approached Louise from behind, grabbed her by the shoulder, and spun her around.

"Ouch. That's the shoulder you injured the other day."

"What do you mean? I never injured you." Delilah looked around, Beth assumed, in hopes that no one was listening.

"When I was trying to help your mother, you pushed me away."

Delilah turned and walked away. Louise looked at Beth. "What a piece of work."

The minister arrived, said some prayers, and left. The music began.

"That's the song I would have chosen if I had the chance," Delilah said contemptuously.

"Mom, please be quiet."

"Don't tell me to be quiet, you be quiet."

As the service ended, friends and family paid their respects to Margaret. Delilah was the only one standing near the coffin, her siblings looking at each other in disbelief.

When everyone except immediate family had left, Beth stood with Edward and their sons. She watched as the funeral director closed the coffin. Beth, along with her Aunt Bertha, Aunt Marie, Uncle Norman, Uncle Brian, and several cousins, were overcome with grief and had to sit down. Delilah stood stiff, head erect, no trace of remorse or hint of a tear.

They made their way to the cemetery where Margaret was laid to rest next to her husband, Joe. Beth was saddened when she realized she lost both of her grandmothers within thirteen months.

As she turned from the grave, she saw Delilah approach Uncle Norman, "Sorry, she won't be living with you anymore." Delilah began laughing.

Beth was stunned.

Chapter 14

A few days after Margaret's funeral, Beth sat alone in her grief. Edward was at work, Jon and Jack were at school, and Joseph was napping. She took this quiet time to reminisce about her grandmother. Tears welled up in her eyes when she heard the doorbell ring. Although she was in no mood for company, she decided if she didn't answer the door, whoever was there might keep ringing the bell and wake up Joseph. She walked down the stairs and opened the door. She gasped as she felt her heart begin to pound inside her chest.

"Mom, what are you doing here?" she asked, her voice shaky from crying.

Delilah had a big smile on her face. "The last time I was here was with your grandmother. I'm glad I don't have to deal with her anymore."

Beth realized that was the last time she saw Margaret alive. She felt grateful that she had given her grandmother a happy peaceful afternoon. Beth suspected that it was the last time her grandma was at peace for the remainder of her life and sighed at the thought.

"I'm on my way to Aunt Clara's, but first I need some coffee. Her coffee tastes like crap."

"I think I have some coffee left," Beth said, making her way to the kitchen. "Why are you going to Aunt Clara's?"

"Now that both of your grandmothers are gone, I have time to help her."

Beth swallowed hard. "Why do you think she needs help? She seems to be functioning fine on her own."

"I just think she needs help. She has nobody else since Uncle John died, and that's just my nature. I help people."

Beth felt nauseated. "She has Joey and Steven and her own family."

"She doesn't need them, she has me."

Beth realized she could not change Delilah's mind, so she just gave up.

Clara was Mike's aunt through marriage. Her husband, John, was Helen's brother. Mike once told Beth he had been close to his Uncle John and Aunt Clara his whole life. They had no children of their own, so they showered Mike and his brother Paul, along with their cousin Steven, with all of their affection. After Joey was born, he was also included.

Beth always felt palpable tension between Delilah and Uncle John. When Beth asked Mike about it, he told her, "Uncle John didn't want me to marry your mother. He said he sensed evil in her. Your mother found out and has hated him all these years."

"Is that why we didn't spend much time with them?"

"Yeah. Your mother didn't want me near him. She thought he would try to convince me to divorce her."

"Wow."

"I feel bad. I stayed with them in Johnston after my parents moved here to Chicago. They did everything for me and now your mother tries to keep me away."

"I'm sure they understand," Beth said while patting her father on the shoulder.

Beth remembered when, two and a half years before Helen's death, Delilah told her, "Last night your father received a phone call from Aunt Clara telling him Uncle John had taken ill and asked for his help. Of course, I went along to help. I would have been there earlier in the day if she would've called me. We drove him to the hospital. The doctors did their examine and said he had a stroke. Serves him right, the son-of-a-bitch.

"Is Daddy okay? How's Aunt Clara? What did you do with Grandma Helen? How's Uncle doing?"

"One question at a time. Your father is fine. Grandma is with Louise this week. I'm glad I didn't have to contend with her with everything else I had to do. Uncle

John is doing better. They say he'll probably make a full recovery, but if he doesn't, Aunt Clara will need my help."

"Tell everyone I'm thinking about them. I'll try to visit Uncle John later this week."

"Don't bother. I've gotta go. I'll call you if I hear anything."

"Okay, goodbye."

Two days later, Beth heard from Mike.

"Your mother just called and told me Uncle John died. She was alone with Uncle in the hospital when he died. She is on her way to bring Aunt Clara to the hospital. I'll talk to you later."

"Okay, Dad thanks for telling me. Give Aunt Clara my sympathies."

"Okay, I will."

Beth thought it strange that Delilah was the only one with Uncle when he died, especially since she had such disdain for him. She also remembered that her mother said the doctors expected a full recovery.

Later that day, Delilah called Beth.

"Uncle John can't tell your father to divorce me now," Delilah giggled, "I'm glad the asshole is dead."

Beth eyes widened in disbelief.

"Aunt Clara is staying with me; she can't be alone. I made all of the funeral arrangements today. The wake will be tomorrow at two and the funeral will be the next day at ten. I'm glad your grandmother is with Louise. I couldn't handle both of them. I told Aunt Clara that even though we haven't been close in the past, we're family and family sticks together."

"Won't Aunt Clara's mother, sister, and brother want to stay with her?"

"I didn't call them, but I told her I did. She won't like them when they don't show up. She'll see I'm the only one she has."

Beth raised her eyebrows. "But Mom, they'll find out and tell Aunt Clara you didn't call them. She should be with her family."

"I'm her family now; the rest of them can go to hell. I'll just tell her they're lying because they didn't want to come."

"Mom, you shouldn't lie."

"What difference does it make? No one knows I'm lying."

"Regardless, you shouldn't lie."

"I don't care."

The following afternoon Beth, Edward, and their three sons arrived at the funeral home. Beth removed her coat while Edward held Joseph, who was only three weeks old. She helped Jon and Jack remove their coats and had them stomp the snow off their boots. She took Joseph and unbundled him. Louise approached Beth.

"Let me see the little munchkin. Oh Beth, he's beautiful." Beth beamed. "I'm so happy for him. He has been born into a loving home. I'm convinced he will be loved and happy."

"Thanks, Louise, he will be."

Delilah was standing near enough to hear the conversation. She walked over.

"Yes, he's beautiful. He looks like his grandmother."

Sarcastic grins spread across everyone's face. Delilah turned and in her loudest voice she said, "Hey everyone, come and see my brand-new grandson. He's beautiful, just like me."

Beth held Joseph in one arm and put her other arm around Jon and Jack as she pulled them close. "Mommy loves both of you." They hugged Beth's leg and smiled. Beth motioned to the boys to follow her. They all walked to Aunt Clara and gave her a hug. She then approached her father. "I'm so sorry, Dad."

"Me too. First my father, now my uncle. Looks like it's up to me to be the head of the family."

"Looks like. You can do it," she said with a wink.

"Let me see my new little buddy. Hi, Joseph." He put his hands on top of Jon and Jack's heads. "Hi, buddies." The boy smiled as wide as they could. "Hi, Grandpa!"

Beth and her family took seats. She looked at Uncle John lying in his casket and remembered how excited he was to meet Joseph just two weeks earlier. She turned to Edward. "I can't believe he went so quickly." Then it struck her. "You know, my mother was with both of my grandfathers shortly before they had strokes, and they died shortly after, while she was alone with them, just like Uncle."

Edward had a look of surprise. "What a coincidence."

Delilah remained at Clara's side. When Mike, Joey, or their cousin, Steven, approached Clara, Delilah would step in front of her. "If you want to talk to her, you can talk to me instead." She would turn to Clara. "Don't worry, I'll protect you."

At the cemetery, after the funeral, Delilah approached Beth.

"I insisted Clara stay with me for a few days. I asked Louise to keep Helen an extra week so I can help Clara. I'm glad she agreed. I have to find out about her bank accounts, her work pension, and if she has any life insurance. I'm sure she has a bundle of money. I need to protect her. Now that Uncle John is gone, I'm all she has."

Beth was exhausted by Delilah's scheming. "That's great, Mom. I've got to go. Joseph needs a nap." Beth turned and walked back to her car where Edward and their sons were waiting. Edward opened her door. She got in and sat down, expelling a large puff of air. She looked at Edward. "Let's go."

א

Beth was glad she didn't hear from Delilah for the remainder of the week. On Sunday, however, Mike and Delilah were at Beth's door. Mike went downstairs to sit with Edward, Jon, and Jack. Joseph was napping while Beth was making dessert for after dinner. Beth made coffee and poured out two cups. She set one on the kitchen table for Delilah and took one down to Mike. Delilah and Beth sat down in chairs around the kitchen table.

"I got all of Clara's information. That son-of-a-bitch has a lot of money. I calculated and recalculated. When that SOB dies, I'll have about half a million dollars."

"You'll have? What about her family and Daddy and Joey and Steven?"

"Why should her family get anything? They didn't even come to Uncle John's funeral."

"That's because you didn't tell them about it."

"Oh well," Delilah said with a sigh, "they probably wouldn't have come anyway."

Just then Mike came upstairs. "Grandma, Jon and Jack wonder where you are. They want to show you their new game."

"Shit. Okay, I'm coming."

Delilah went downstairs by the boys. Mike stayed upstairs with Beth, he was shaking.

"Beth, she's doing it again, just like she did with my mother."

"What is she doing, Dad?"

"She took Aunt Clara to all of her banks and had my name put on the accounts. She told Aunt Clara she had to do that in case Clara got sick and I needed money to pay her bills. Your mother also had my name put on Aunt Clara's pension and life insurance as beneficiary. She forced me to sign even though I was reluctant. She's mad at Aunt Clara because she included Joey and Steven in her will. She's relentless. She keeps telling Aunt Clara to take them out of the will. I don't know how to stop her."

Clara and her husband always felt that since they didn't have children, they would leave everything to the nephews in the family. John believed that since the husband was the primary bread winner, *his* money should go to *his* family, so only Mike, Steven, and Joey would be mentioned in their will.

Delilah walked up the stairs. "What the hell are you two talking about?"

Beth stood up. "Joseph will be four weeks old Tuesday. Time sure flies."

Mike turned to walk back downstairs. Beth reached out and hugged him.

"I love you, Dad."

"I love you too, Beth."

Beth and Delilah sat down. "So Mom, what else have you been up to?"

"Well," Delilah sat erect, tossing back her head, "I took that SOB to my attorney."

"Is that the same attorney you took Grandma Helen to?"

"Yeah, he did a good job for Grandma, I'm sure he'll do the same for Clara."

"I'm sure," Beth thought, *or for you.*

"Yeah, but I'm mad at him. He made me leave the room while he talked to Aunt Clara. When they finished, he called me in to witness. I saw she had Joey and Steven in the will."

"Well, they are her nephews."

"Yeah, but since Uncle John died, I'm the only one who does anything for her. I'm sure Joey and Steven will only come around to see what they can get. I need to protect her."

"I don't think Joey or Steven want anything."

"Well, I asked her what they have been doing for her, how she can dare include them. I'm the only one who helps her."

"Uncle John just died; they are probably giving her time to grieve. I'm sure they'll help her if she needs something."

"They can all go to hell. She doesn't need them."

Beth had grown weary. "Whatever."

As she finished her coffee, Delilah rose from the chair. "I'm taking her to see Doctor Cube. I don't like what her doctor is telling her. He keeps telling her she's healthy. I know she's not healthy. I want to see what Doctor Cube says."

Delilah walked out of the room. Beth followed her.

"Let's go, Mike!" Delilah yelled down the steps.

As Delilah walked out the door, Beth felt relief that she was gone but felt sadness for Aunt Clara.

Delilah phoned Beth the next day.

"Doctor Cube, that asshole, said Clara was in excellent health. She's strong, with a healthy heart, and should live a long time. Son-of-a-bitch."

Beth couldn't listen. "Thanks for letting me know. I'm cooking dinner; I have to go, goodbye."

Beth knew that as with Helen and Margaret, Delilah didn't want to hear that Aunt Clara was healthy, since she couldn't wait for her to die.

Chapter 15

Beth was disheartened by Delilah's treatment of Clara. Clara had never been strong-willed, and since the loss of her husband, she had become unduly vulnerable. Delilah took full advantage of this vulnerability. Beth observed the grip of Delilah's control become tighter and tighter.

Often when Mike and Delilah would visit Beth, Clara would accompany them. During one of these visits Clara waited for Delilah to leave the room, then confided in Beth.

"The other day, when I went out to dinner with my friend, I returned to find your mother sitting on the front steps. Your mother began to scream at me, asking me how I dare go to dinner with someone else. Your mother said she was the only one that does anything for me, therefore,

I should spend all of my time with her, no one else." Clara began to wring her hands. "She said other people only want to use me, they really don't care about me. While my friend was standing next to me, your mother asked who paid the bill. When I said I did, your mother threw up her arms and said, there you go. My friend shook her head and said she didn't need this and walked away. My friend has not spoken to me since."

"I'm so sorry. Have you spoken to your family? Maybe they can help."

Clara looked down at the floor. "When I tell Delilah that I have spoken to my mother or sister, she screams at me, telling me they weren't around when I needed them so I don't need them now. Once, my sister called while your mother was at my house. Your mother pushed the receiver down and the call was disconnected. She forbids me to speak to my family."

Beth was horrified, although she was used to Delilah's behavior, she felt this was over the edge.

"You really shouldn't allow her to control you. If you let her have her way, she will continue to ruin your other relationships."

"She keeps telling me if I don't, she won't ever help me again, and when I need help, I'll have no one."

"She doesn't really mean it. Besides, you can always call me, Joey, or Louise. We'll help you."

"No Beth, I wouldn't want her to get mad at you. I don't think Joey will help me anymore either." Beth

141

heard sorrow in Clara's voice. "Your mother dropped in last week. Joey was at my house. He was taking down my drapes for me so I could have them cleaned. Your mother began to scream at Joey, telling him he had no business being there. She again told me that if I let others help me, she would not help me. He left without taking down the drapes. He didn't even say goodbye. I think he is finished helping me. It was so much easier when John was here."

"I'm sorry my mother treats you so badly, but I'll help you. I'm used to my mother screaming. It doesn't bother me, except for her cursing around my children. You can call me."

"Thanks, Beth."

Clara took a step forward and gave Beth a hug. Delilah saw them as she walked out from the kitchen. "What's that about?"

Beth smiled at Delilah. "Just being friends."

After they left, Beth began to think about the situation. Delilah was deliberately pushing Clara's friends and family out of her life; it was one more way for Delilah to be in control.

Clara told Beth she also had doubts about Delilah's true intentions, but she didn't want to get on Delilah's bad side. She hoped that since Mike and Delilah had their vacation home in Johnston, Delilah would not object to her traveling with them so she could see her family.

Clara was born in South Dakota and moved to Johnston as a young teenager. Clara's father died while they lived in South Dakota. Her mother remarried, and her new husband decided to move the family to Johnston. Johnston was a logging community with plenty of employment opportunities. It also had an abundance of fertile farmland and numerous lakes with unlimited supply of fish for food. Clara's stepfather bought a farm outside of town, where he could keep his new family secluded. He took a job with a logging company, which left Clara, her sister, and her mother responsible for maintaining the farm. Clara shared stories with Beth about the abuse that was inflicted upon her by her stepfather. Beth understood what it felt like to be abused, so Clara and Beth had a special bond.

Clara met her husband while they were both in high school. John played the accordion in the school band, and they sometimes played at other locations throughout town. John was quite handsome, his dark brown hair always in a crew cut. He had mischievous brown eyes, which appeared more mischievous by the mustache that John had always sported. Clara always talked about how much she loved listening to John play. However, because of her duties on the farm, it didn't allow her much time to spend with John. Although he was two years ahead of her, he was smitten. Clara had a small stature, big brown eyes, and jet black hair, which she always kept tightly curled. She was very pretty as a girl; however, she was quite shy. They dated for two years while Clara was still in high school, but only when Clara's stepfather allowed it. After

Clara graduated, they were married. They bought a small farm and continued to live in Johnston for many years. Clara's mother, sister, and brother still lived in Johnston.

Mike and Delilah did take Clara to Johnston with them when they went to their vacation home, so Clara called her family and told them where she was, hoping they would visit her at Mike and Delilah's house or pick her up and bring her to their home. But Delilah would not allow Clara's family to visit and threatened to call the police if they came into her driveway.

Late one morning, in early autumn, when Jon and Jack had returned to school, Clara called Beth and asked to meet her for lunch. Beth invited Clara to her home, and Clara gladly accepted. When they finished lunch, Beth put Joseph down for his nap. Clara told Beth she took the afternoon off work, and asked if she could stay and talk. Beth poured two cups of coffee and they went into the living room to chat.

"My sister called me. She told me that she and my mother are afraid for me. She told me your mother is too controlling and they wonder what would happen if I went against your mother's demands. She suggested I get a place of my own in Johnston, then they could visit me without your mother's interference. Joey told me how abusive your mother was to both of your grandmothers. I'm afraid she'll abuse me. I don't know what to do."

Beth exhaled. "I don't know either. I agree, you must be careful. Will your family support you if you buy your own place? Why don't you ask Joey and Steven their opinions?"

"I don't know if Joey will talk to me. I think he is mad at me for asking him to remove my drapes."

"Joey is upset with my mother, not with you. Would you like me to ask him to call you?"

"Would you? You can find out if he's angry with me."

"I'll do that. Would you like me to call Steven too?"

"No, let's just start with Joey."

"Okay, I'll call him tonight."

"Thanks, Beth, I feel better now." Beth could hear the joy in Clara's voice.

"I'm glad."

That evening, after Beth put her children to bed, she telephoned Joey as she had promised. She relayed the story and everyone's fears. He was also afraid for Clara and thought something must be done. He agreed to call her. An hour later, Joey phoned Beth back.

"Aunt Clara and I agreed, the only way she will be allowed to see her family is to have her own place. I'll take her to Johnston this weekend to look around."

"I agree, she needs to get away from my mother, that's the only way she'll be able to see anyone else," Beth said. "She's just afraid of telling my mother, and she doesn't know how to do it. Maybe she can say she wants to give my parents some freedom. If she has her own place, they won't have to take her with them."

"That's a good idea. I'll tell her that on our way to Johnston. Thanks Beth."

"Let me know if I can help."

א

The following Monday Joey phoned Beth to update her on their trip.

"Aunt Clara saw a two-acre parcel of land directly across the road from the farm my mother and Uncle John grew up on. She felt it was meant to be. She signed a purchase agreement and decided if she gets the land, she will put a mobile home on it. We stopped and looked at some on our way home. There is one in particular that she really likes. She's so excited."

"I'm glad you did that with her. She needs to rely on you and Steven more. Maybe then my mother will back off."

"That's what Aunt Clara hopes too."

א

Wednesday that week, Clara telephoned Beth.

"Did you talk to Joey?"

"Yes, on Monday."

"Did he tell you about the land I found?"

"He did. It sounds perfect!"

"I found out this morning that I got it. I was so

excited I phoned and ordered the mobile home I wanted. I'll send them a check tomorrow. As soon as they get my check, they'll deliver the mobile home."

"That's great, when do you expect to be in your new home?"

"Well," she said after taking a deep breath, "I told your mother. She was fit to be tied. She is not happy with me, of course. She said I did this behind her back and that I had no right including Joey in my decision. The decision should have been hers to make."

"No, Aunt Clara, the decision is yours to make."

"That's what I told her, but that just made her more upset. I'm proud of the decision I made."

"So am I. You're beginning to stand up for yourself and make your own choices. Uncle would be proud of you too."

Clara began to sob. "Thank you for saying that. I'll be able to look out my front window every day and imagine him running through the fields he ran through as a young boy. Oh Beth, I'm so happy."

"I'm happy for you, too. So when do you move in?"

"Well, I have to have them dig a well and run electricity, but I should be able to get that done next week. So I'm hoping I'll be in my new place within three weeks. I'm so excited, except your mother demanded that she still has to watch out for my best interests, so she insisted that she and Mike be there when my mobile home is delivered. Now, I'm back to revolving around her schedule."

147

"Well, keep your chin up. Once you have your mobile home, you should have more freedom."

"Let's hope so."

Chapter 16

Clara spent that Christmas with Beth, Edward, and the boys. She came with Mike and Delilah. Mike went downstairs to sit with Edward, while Delilah went into the kitchen to help herself to a cup of coffee. Beth and Clara went to sit in the living room. Clara was in an unusually good mood. "I went to see Doctor Cube a few days ago. He said I was in excellent health. He thought I should live twenty more years."

"I'm glad you're doing well. I hope you live more than twenty years!" Beth said "We all enjoy having you with us. Do you see Doctor Cube all the time or do you still go to your own doctor?"

"No, your mother doesn't let me go to my own doctor, she only allows me to see Doctor Cube. I enjoy being with you too Beth, but I have a strange feeling."

"What do you mean?" Beth asked with concern.

Clara grew somber. "I can't help feeling this will be my last Christmas."

"Aunt Clara," Beth was stunned, "how can you think that? The doctor said you will live twenty more years."

"I know, but I have a feeling..."

Beth didn't like what Clara was saying so she changed the subject. "How do you like your new mobile home?"

"I enjoy my time there. It gives me comfort to know that your Uncle John used to walk, and play and chop wood on the farm that's right across the road. I feel close to him when I'm there. I remember meeting his family there for the first time. Busha, Uncle's mother, made dinner and invited Aunt Katherine, Uncle Steven, your grandparents and all the kids. It was wonderful. In fact that's where I first met your father.

"Now I sit in my front window looking at the farm and remember all the stories Uncle told me. It gives me great comfort. The mobile home is wonderful. It has a big kitchen, with plenty of cabinets and a built-in China cabinet for my dishes. The living room is also very large. It was supposed to have three bedrooms, but I had them turn the smaller bedrooms into one large master bedroom. It sits on a piece of land that I had cleared so it's surrounded by forest, except for the farm across the road. All I see when I look out my back or side windows are trees.

Last time I was out there, I noticed some choke cherry trees. If I'm still here in the spring, I want to go up there and pick the cherries to make wine. Sometimes I see the deer inching into the clearing. They're so beautiful. And I hear the coyotes at night. I love leaving my windows open at night. The breeze blows across me and scents my bedroom with the smell of pine. I bet the air will really smell like pine in the winter."

"I'm glad you find comfort there, Aunt Clara."

Delilah walked into the living room, carrying her cup of coffee.

"Humph," was all Delilah could say.

Jon, Jack, and Joseph ran upstairs and into the living room.

"Time for presents!" they all yelled.

"Okay, okay, hold your horses." Beth loved seeing the excitement in her sons' faces.

The group walked downstairs where the Christmas tree stood surrounded by presents.

As they reached the bottom of the stairs and headed into the family room, Clara stopped and put her hand up to her mouth.

"It's beautiful. An old-fashioned Christmas, just like the ones we had in South Dakota. Beth, I have not seen bubble lights on a Christmas tree in thirty years. You have so many beautiful, old-fashioned ornaments. I haven't seen those in many years either. Seems nowadays, everybody wants everything new and shiny. Where did you find all of those ornaments?"

"Some were my grandmother's and some were Edwards' grandmother's."

Beth took Clara by the elbow and walked over to the tree. They stood together while Beth touched each ornament and explained its origin.

Clara reached up and touched one. "I remember my mother having one just like this when I was a little girl. I miss those times."

"Jon, would you like to pass out the presents? Where are Daddy and Grandpa?"

"I'll get them." Jack ran through the room as fast as he could and opened the door to the garage. "Presents!" he yelled.

Edward, Mike, and Jack returned with Jack pulling his father's arm.

Beth looked at Edward, "Fire, Daddy?"

Edward started a fire in the fireplace. Beth loved hearing the crackle of the logs and the smell of the wood burning. Jon continued on his mission of passing out presents, instructing, "Dad, you sit here, this is your pile," motioning to the chair next to the fireplace. "Grandpa, over here," leading Mike to the sofa. "Jack, sit by me."

Beth giggled. "Bossy son of a gun."

Edward, Mike, and Clara laughed. Delilah busied herself counting how many packages each person had. They went around the room, taking turns opening presents. Beth came to a package marked from Aunt Clara and Uncle John. Beth was surprised.

"Aunt Clara, you didn't have to get me anything."

"I know I didn't have to, I wanted to."

Beth unwrapped the package to find three sets of Christmas plates, patterned with a Christmas tree laden with presents. "Aunt Clara, these are beautiful, thank you so much."

Beth rose from her seat and walked over to Clara, giving her a hug.

"You're welcome. I hope you keep these until your boys get married. Give each of them a set. When you use them, think of me and Uncle."

"I will. What a wonderful tradition you have started for us."

"Just remember this last Christmas we spent together."

Beth looked at Clara with sadness. *Why does she keep thinking this is her last Christmas?*

Delilah spoke up. "Aunt Clara is coming to Johnston with us tomorrow."

Clara looked sorrowful. "I don't like driving in the winter, so I'm riding with your parents."

"Well, I hope you have a safe trip."

Edward sniffed the air. "I'm beginning to salivate. That prime rib smells great. I bet it's time to eat. Let's go up."

Everyone followed Edward up the stairs, and they

all sat around the dining room table, Christmas carols playing gently in the background.

After dinner the men and the boys went downstairs to play with their new toys. Clara and Delilah helped Beth cleanup and wash dishes. When everything was cleaned, the three of them went to sit in the living room.

Beth noticed a tear in Clara's eye. "Aunt Clara, what's wrong?"

"This has been one of the happiest Christmases of my life. You have made me feel so welcomed and loved. The only thing that could have made it better is Uncle being here. Thank you so much for such a wonderful day."

"You're welcome, Aunt Clara. I'll try to make next year even better."

"No Beth, this one was great." Clara wiped a tear from her cheek.

Joseph ran upstairs. "More cookies, please."

Beth fixed two plates of cookies. She placed one on the living room coffee table for Delilah and Clara and took the other downstairs, along with coffee and eggnog.

Clara picked up a glass of eggnog. "I love eggnog. Uncle used to make it for me from scratch. When I was a little girl, when my father was still alive, he would make milk punch. I really enjoyed that too. I don't know how he made it but it was good. Once my mother married my stepfather, Christmases weren't so much fun anymore. I don't think my stepfather liked me very much. The only presents I would get for Christmas were socks and underwear. We never had much of tree, just branches that might have fallen off in the snow."

Clara looked up and glanced out the window. "The snow sure is pretty. I hope the roads are clear tomorrow."

When everyone was finished, Delilah announced it was time to leave. "We need to get an early start. Johnston is a long way. Clara is spending the night. She's been with us for a week."

Beth looked puzzled as she asked Aunt Clara. "Why have you spent the week with my parents?"

Clara looked sullen as she responded, "I don't have my car, and they won't take me home."

As they were leaving, Clara gave Beth a hug. "Goodbye Beth. Thank you for such a beautiful day."

"You're welcome. Thank you for the beautiful plates. Stay safe."

Clara kissed Beth on the cheek, squeezed her hand, turned, and walked toward the door. As Clara picked up her purse, Beth noticed a large bundle of cash. The top bill was a one hundred dollar bill so, to Beth, it looked like several thousand dollars.

צ

Beth hadn't heard anything from Delilah, Mike, or Clara for the whole week, until late afternoon on New Year's Eve.

Beth answered the telephone. It was her mother.

"Well, it will be a happy New Year. This asshole is dead."

Beth trembled. "Mom, who's dead?"

"Clara."

"How can she be dead?" Beth said in shock. "What happened?"

"All the way up here, she kept insisting we take her to her place. I got sick of listening to her. I told your father to bring her to our house. She kept talking about Joey and Steven and how Uncle asshole wanted everything divided between them and your father. Why the hell should either of those assholes get anything? What do they do for her?"

"Mom, how did Aunt Clara die?"

"She kept asking your father to take her to her mobile home. She couldn't walk there because it was too far in the cold and snow. I told your father not to take her. I told her last night we would be coming home today. Then this morning she didn't get up at her usual five a.m. Your father wanted to check on her, but I told him to let her sleep. I did my exercises and cleaned up to get ready to go. I made lunch and told your father check on her. He came back into the kitchen, frantic, saying he thought Clara was dead."

Beth gasped.

"I went in to check on her. She was cold and stiff. I got a mirror from the bathroom and held it under her nose. She wasn't breathing. Your father and I ate lunch, then he helped me lay her on the floor so I could change the sheets. He helped me take off Clara's pajamas, and I put everything in the washer. I washed her, put one of my nightgowns on her, and put clean sheets on the bed. We lifted her off the floor, placed her in bed, made her look comfortable, and called the coroner."

Beth thought it strange that Delilah was so calm. She did not detect one bit of remorse in Delilah's voice and suspected Delilah hadn't even shed a tear.

"How's Daddy?"

"He's fine. I cleaned the kitchen and made sure I cleaned everything up after washing Clara. I didn't want to give any bad impressions. I asked the coroner if anything looked suspicious, but he didn't answer. All he said was that it was heart failure."

Beth was breathless. Just one week ago Doctor Cube told Clara to expect to live another twenty years. Now she was gone. Clara was right, that was her last Christmas.

Chapter 17

Aunt Clara's wake was held in Johnston. Since Johnston was an eight hour drive from Chicago, Beth and her son, Jack, had flown into town to attend. Jon and Joseph both had the flu, so Edward stayed home with them.

During the wake, Jack told Beth he was hungry. The restaurant was only two and a half blocks away so Beth decided they would walk to town for dinner. Beth approached her Aunt Louise to ask if Cooper, Louise's son, might go with them. He was around Jack's age so Beth thought Jack would enjoy his company. Aunt Louise agreed he could come along. Both boys were so bundled up for the weather, Beth giggled at them and told them they looked like colorful marshmallow men. The boys started poking at each other with their mittened-hands, calling each other marshmallow man. The sight brought a smile to Beth's face.

Beth felt her father's gentle hand grabbing her arm. "Where are you going?"

"I'm taking the boys to dinner."

"It is too dark for you to walk alone. Wait while I ask your mother if I can go with you."

As Beth and the two boys waited at the door, Beth was pensive, shaking her head in disbelief as she watched Mike approach her mother, Delilah.

Delilah was busy being her usual center of attention, making rounds, hugging everyone in the room, all the while sobbing as if she was in significant pain, as if she was sad that Aunt Clara had died. As she noticed Mike walking towards her, Delilah's sobs ceased. Her gimlet eyes peered at Mike as she struck a pose of superiority, straightening to an erect posture, while placing her hands on her hips.

She rolled her cold eyes as she snapped, "What do you want now?"

"I would like to walk Beth and the boys to town. The boys are hungry and it is too dark for them to walk alone. Can I go with them?"

Delilah shrieked, "I don't care what you do; can't you see I'm busy here?"

As Mike turned toward Beth and the boys, he heard

Delilah, as did Beth, mumble under her breath, "I can't stand this. Can't you do anything on your own? Do I have to make all your decisions for you?"

As her father drew nearer, Beth saw the wounded look in his beautiful brown eyes as he gently wiped away a tear. His head dropped in sorrow. "If I made my own decisions, without consulting your mother, I would have hell to pay."

Beth gently touched his arm. "I'm sorry, Dad." Beth knew very well what Mike was dealing with. "I understand. You know that she has done that to me my whole life. Even now that I'm married with children of my own, she stills expects me to ask her permission for anything I do. I'm sorry she does that to you too." Mike patted Beth's arm and they headed out the door

The snow was gently falling as they stepped outside and crunched under their feet as they walked along. The sky was dark and full of stars, and although the air was brisk, there was a full moon, which seemed to warm them as they walked. The funeral home was just one block from Main Street, which was only three blocks long. The restaurant Beth had decided to go to was in the middle of town, so they only had two and a half blocks to walk. As they were walking, the boys commented on how the snowflakes sparkled as they fell in front of the streetlights. The two boys giggled while trying to catch them on their tongues and laughed out loud when the snowflakes stuck to their eyelashes.

"We have eyes like frosty," they giggled, their faces beaming. The boys ran ahead, pretending they were ice-skating. Beth and her father were enjoying the Christmas lights and decorations on the homes, commenting to each other that Aunt Clara would be happy to know they were able to find enjoyment among all of their sorrow. Beth relayed the story Aunt Clara told her about candle lights in windows signaling a welcome to baby Jesus on his birthday. Beth turned her head to look at the boys when she saw a snowball coming her way. The two boys roared with laughter as Beth jumped with surprise just as the snowball hit. Beth and her father joined in the laughter as they returned the snowballs.

As the foursome made their way, they began to smell the enticing aroma coming from the restaurant, welcoming everybody in. They sat in a booth by the window so the boys could watch the snow and enjoy the decorations on the storefronts. The windows were encir-cled by colorful old-fashioned bulb lights and decorated with designs made by wiping glass wax into plastic sten-cils. After they placed their order, the boys carried on with their giggles and began a conversation that only the two of them understood. Beth's face beamed with delight at the fun they were having. Beth turned back toward her father as he gazed off into the distance, his brow furrowed.

"What's wrong, Dad?"

"I was just thinking, I can't wait for this funeral

to be over so I can get back to Clara's house to find her will. Two weeks ago she told me she had written a letter and attached it to her will. She said the letter explained she wanted me to have all of her money and property; Steven and Joey were not to get anything. That's what your mother has been trying to force Clara to do. If I find that letter, maybe your mother will get off my back."

Beth froze. "Two weeks," she said in a whisper. Those two small words hit her like a sledgehammer. She remembered where she heard them and the implication of what they meant sent a chill down her spine.

Mike noticed the change in Beth's face. "Are you all right?"

Beth shook the thought out of her head. She couldn't think about that now, not at Clara's funeral. And she didn't want to get her father upset. He had to put up with so much already.

Beth plastered a smile on her face. "I'm fine, Dad. Really."

As they left the restaurant to journey back to the funeral home, Beth was hit with the sickening sweet smell of the vapors spewing from the smoke stack of the hardboard factory that sat on the edge of town, and it made her sick to her stomach. She wondered if it was the smell that was making her sick or the recognition of those two words: two weeks.

The two boys resumed their fun, frolicking through

the snow in what Beth would normally consider a winter wonderland. But thinking about the meaning behind "two weeks," nothing seemed wonderful anymore.

Beth had a sudden urge to be with Edward. Her body ached for his strong yet gentle arms to envelop her and draw her near, while assuring her everything would be okay. Right now she wasn't so sure that was the case.

Chapter 18

Delilah insisted Joey, Louise, and Cooper, along with Beth and Jack, all stay in their vacation home while attending Aunt Clara's wake and funeral.

After the funeral, when everyone was back in Delilah's home, Louise began to ask questions. The two young boys were already sleeping for the night. It had been an emotional day for everybody.

"Delilah, did Aunt Clara have a will? I sure hope she did. Since she didn't have any children, that's the only way anyone would know her wishes."

As had been witnessed numerous times through the years, Delilah began to shake and roll her hands into fists. Then she started flailing her arms and stamping her feet as her face became a bright shade of red.

"What the hell do you care?" she yelled. "It's none

of your business. Why should you expect anything from her? What the hell have you ever done for her?"

"I'm not expecting anything." Louise was shaking, tears in her eyes. "Why are you yelling at me? I just want to make sure Aunt Clara's wishes are carried out."

"I'll worry about this son-of-a-bitch's wishes. You worry about yourself. Maybe you should worry about working on your marriage."

Louise started to sob. "My marriage is fine and has nothing to do with this conversation."

Delilah's eyes pierced Louise. "Go to hell."

Delilah jammed her finger into Louise's shoulder, causing Louise to lose her balance. Since they were standing in the kitchen, Louise was able to grab onto the counter to stop herself from falling. Delilah continued poking at Louise, screaming, "This conversation is none of your business. You're just an in-law."

"So are you."

"You son-of-a-bitch." Delilah turned to Joey. "Get her out of here before I kill her."

Delilah moved to the back door and opened it. She grabbed Louise by the back of her shirt, putting her body up against Louise's, and pushed her towards the door. It was January and extremely cold. The snow had once again begun to fall, adding to the six inches already on the ground. Joey stood up but couldn't move fast enough to reach his wife in time. When Delilah got to the door, she put her foot in the small of Louise's back and kicked her out the door. Louise fell into the cold, deep snow. Joey immediately ran for his son, grabbed him out of bed, and while cradling him in his arms ran out of the kitchen door. None of them had on shoes or coats.

Luckily, Joey still had his car keys in his pants pocket. He was able to unlock the car door and allow Louise and Cooper to get in out of the snow. Joey then went back to the house. He opened the back door and looked inside until he spotted Mike.

"Mike would you please bring our coats and shoes?"

"Sure, come in out of the cold."

Joey stepped inside.

As Mike was gathering their coats and shoes, Delilah came to the door with their luggage, pushed Joey aside with her hip, and began to hurl the luggage out the door. When Mike returned, Joey put on his coat and shoes, went outside to give Louise her coat and shoes, and covered Cooper with his coat. He then took their luggage, which was now covered in snow, put it in the trunk of their car, and headed for home.

Beth worried that Joey and Louise had an eight hour ride in front of them, afraid it would be made longer by the slick roads caused by the heavy snow. In addition to the emotions of Clara's funeral, and the horror she had just witnessed at Delilah's hands, Beth was devastated.

After they had left, Delilah started to laugh hysterically. "I hope they will crash and die before ever reaching home."

Beth started crying. "Please don't say that."

"If they die, I won't have to share any of Clara's money with them. I'll have it all to myself except for asshole Steven."

"Having money isn't worth someone's life."

"Who the hell has been lying to you?"

Beth couldn't take it anymore; she turned from Delilah and looked at Mike. "Good night, Dad. I'll see you in the morning."

"Don't you say good night to me, too?" Delilah asked.

Beth looked at her mother and shook her head in disbelief. She couldn't believe her mother still wanted recognition after what she just did to Joey and Louise's family.

"Good night," she said, without emotion.

Beth walked into the bedroom and closed the door. She was unable to fall asleep, worrying about Joey, Louise, and Cooper. She was also glad that Jack did not wake up. She didn't want him to witness his grandmother's violence.

The next day Delilah decided to return home. Beth and her son rode back with them. Beth was somber as a result of Clara's death and what she had witnessed the night before. Beth kept telling Mike that she was anxious to get home.

"I miss my family and want to get home to them." But she silently thought, *I'm also anxious to get away from my mother.* She was afraid that she and Jack may also become victims of Delilah's anger, as Beth had been so many times before. Instead of taking Beth home, Mike and Delilah went to Clara's. Delilah ran into Clara's bedroom and began opening all of the dresser drawers, and like a mad woman, she threw whatever was in the drawers up into the air. She then did the same thing with the nightstands and chest of drawers. When she didn't find what she was looking for, Delilah began to mumble to herself and throw things out of the closet.

When Clara's bedroom was a total shambles, Delilah went into the second bedroom and performed the same ritual. Delilah suddenly stopped, turned towards Mike and Beth, and showed the most evil looking smile Beth had ever seen, her yellow teeth protruding over her gums. Delilah lifted her hand and opened it, revealing a stack of cash. She sat on the floor and counted out forty thousand dollars.

"I'll be able to have a good time now."

Delilah stuck the money into her pocket and walked into the kitchen. She started opening cabinet doors and drawers pushing things from side to side on her quest for treasure. Beth's mood turned gloomy as she remembered visiting Aunt Clara and Uncle John and how careful Aunt Clara had been with the figurines she kept on her kitchen windowsill. They were now being broken as Delilah rampaged through the kitchen. When she found nothing there, Delilah went into the living room. She began to push furniture out of the way. She even rolled up the rug that was in the center of the room. She moved tables and large cabinets in her search for anything valuable. Beth was astonished at the strength Delilah possessed. After approximately two hours, Beth had finally convinced Mike to take her home.

While on the way to Beth's home, Delilah became agitated. "Drive faster. I have to get back to asshole's house to find her will." Delilah exhaled. "Two weeks ago Clara told me that she had written a codicil to her will, removing Joey and Steven and leaving everything to us." When they arrived at Beth's home, Mike went to the trunk to remove Beth's luggage while Beth and Jack got out of the car. Delilah refused to come in for some coffee and refused even to get out of the car. She was determined to get back to Clara's house and find the will.

⚐

The following day Delilah filled Beth in on the rest of what she had found.

"While I was looking for the will, I found an additional forty thousand dollars behind Clara's refrigerator. I'm so happy! Now I have eighty thousand dollars to do whatever I want with. And your father, Joey, and Steven aren't entitled to any of the money because I'm the one who found it." She began to laugh. "I'm anxious to get

169

back to Clara's house since I haven't found the will yet. I want to find it so I can get my money."

Beth heard from her again later that day.

"Your father found the will. I'm so pissed. If Clara wasn't dead I would kill her. She did not remove Joey and Steven."

It seemed to Beth that the fox had been outfoxed. She was glad Delilah had called and not stopped by with her news. Beth couldn't help but grin.

"Your father and I will be cleaning out all of Clara's bank accounts today before Joey or Steven find out about them. And then we have to get her pension and life insurance too."

Beth just shook her head in disgust.

Chapter 19

The day after Beth returned from Clara's funeral, after the children left for school, Beth sat quietly, curled up, covered with a down lap throw, on her living room sofa. As she sipped a cup of herbal tea, she glanced out the window to watch the snow gently falling. She tried to forget the horrors of the previous day, but the memories kept flooding back to her.

Although she knew that Delilah was evil and had a very bad temper, she could not believe all she had witnessed. *Knowing and believing are not the same thing. I can't believe she did this.*

Beth got up from the sofa and went to her telephone. She wanted to make sure Joey, Louise, and Cooper arrived home safely. She wanted to call sooner, but by the time she returned home the day before, it was too late to call. Beth was thankful that Louise answered the telephone.

"I was so worried about you, Joey, and Cooper. I'm glad you're home safe and sound."

"No thanks to your mother. It took us twenty-two hours to get home."

Beth inhaled sharply. "What? It's an eight hour drive. I expected a couple of extra hours for the weather, but twenty-two hours, holy cow."

"The weather was pretty bad. The roads were slick and Joey drove slowly, he wouldn't let me drive. He said the roads were slippery and driving was tough. It started to snow heavily so it was difficult to see where the road was. Joey was upset by what your mother had done and very tired. The heavy snow made him drowsier. He even fell asleep. Luckily I saw him drop off and I called out to him, waking him up."

Louise's voice was trembling. "I was so scared. We hit a patch of ice and Joey lost control. The car swerved and spun in circles." Louise began to cry. "I believed we were all going to crash and die."

"Oh Louise, I'm so sorry."

"We crashed head-on into the ditch. Luckily, no one was hurt."

"Thank God."

"That's not the half of it. Joey tried to back out of the ditch but the car was wedged into the snow. Joey wanted to walk for help, but I told him with the heavy snow and the darkness, drivers wouldn't see him. Also, I didn't see a house in sight, and since it was the middle of the night, no one would get out of bed and answer the door, even if he did find a house. The next town was twelve miles, he couldn't walk that far in the cold dark and none of the businesses would be open, anyway. He finally agreed to stay put. We slept in the cold car until the state trooper found us in the morning."

Beth sniffled. "How horrible. How did you get out? Did the trooper call a tow truck?"

"Yeah, but we had to wait three hours. Cooper was crying, he was so cold and hungry. I was grateful that the trooper drove us into the next town. We went into a restaurant to get warm and eat breakfast. We sat there until the trooper came back to get us. Beth, it was horrible."

Beth sighed, "I can't even imagine. It sounds terrible."

"It was."

"Louise, I'm so sorry, I wish I could have done something to stop my mother."

"No one can stop her."

"Well, if there's anything I can do, let me know. I'm glad everyone is okay."

"Me too. I'll talk to you soon."

Beth hung up the phone. She was overcome with sadness. She felt terrible that Joey and Louise had suffered so much as a result of Delilah's anger. Beth also felt sorry for herself because Delilah was her mother.

Beth whispered to herself, "Please don't ever let me be like her. "

Just as she put the receiver back into its cradle, the telephone rang again. She heard Delilah on the other end.

"I've been trying to call you. Who the hell have you been talking to?"

"Louise and Joey had a very difficult drive home. They went in the ditch and had to sleep in their cold car."

Delilah began to laugh. "Too bad they didn't die. If Joey would have died, I would have had his share of Clara's money."

Beth took a deep breath to try and calm herself so she wouldn't yell at her mother. She knew from experience that would not get her anywhere. "What did you call for, Mom?"

"I'm going shopping. Do you want to go with?"

"No Mom, I have things to do here."

"You can talk to Louise all day, but you can't go out with me?"

"Mom, I gotta go."

As Beth hung up the phone, it again became evident that Delilah only cared about herself. She had no regard for how her actions might affect others.

Beth went back into the living room and sat back down on the sofa to finish her tea. Once again her mind began to wonder. She thought about the joy the two boys had while walking in the snow on their way to dinner. That thought brought a smile to her face and she felt a glimmer of happiness, something she had not been able to feel for several weeks. Then all of a sudden she re-called her father's words: "I'm in a rush for all this to be over with, because two weeks ago, Clara said Joey and Steven are no longer in the will, everything will be left to me."

Those words: *two weeks,* stuck in her head.

As she thought about what her father had said, the dark cloud of doom overcame her. She began to tremble and feel an urgent sense of fear. She realized those were the words Delilah used when replaying the conversation she had with Doctor Cube. "Helen should be dead of heart failure in two weeks."

Her fear intensified. She remembered that Helen had died just two weeks after Delilah made that comment, that Margaret had been with Delilah only two weeks when she had died, and that Mike told Beth that Clara changed her will two weeks before she had died.

Could it be true? Beth froze in fear. *What should I do?* She thought, pressing her hand to her mouth. *Who can I trust?*

Then Beth remembered Delilah's threats of taking her children away. Beth was afraid that if she took her suspicions to the authorities, and Delilah found out, she would try to take her children away. Beth feared that no-body would believe her once they talked to Delilah.

She was able to deceive the social service people

with Helen; maybe she could convince them I abuse my children too.

Just then, the telephone rang again. Beth thought it was Delilah calling to gloat. She was surprised to hear Katherine's voice, Grandma Helen's sister.

"You know, Beth, I was just thinking, when I'm ready to die, I'll just go live with your mother."

"What do you mean?"

"It just occurred to me, everyone seems to die when they go to live with your mother. So when I decide I'm ready to die, I'll go live with her too."

"You can't be serious."

"Yes Beth, I am. I'm convinced that's where people go to die."

Beth now realized the fear of doing nothing was far greater than any other fear she felt.

Chapter 20

Delilah still wasn't happy. She wanted one of Clara's cars for her personal use, yet refused to allow Joey to purchase Clara's other car for Louise to use. Since Mike was the executor of Clara's will, he was able to sign the title of Clara's car over to Delilah for one dollar, stating that since it was an old car, it had no value. In fact, it was a collector car and extremely valuable.

Mike and Delilah spent a lot of time in Clara's home, yet would not allow Joey, Louise, or Steven to enter. Delilah decided what she wanted and took it, yet when anyone else requested any of Clara's things, Delilah would say she couldn't find it. Approximately four months after Clara's death, after Delilah had taken everything she wanted, she allowed Joey and Steven into the home to take what they wanted. She then forced the two of them to help her conduct a sale of the items that were left over, telling them if they wanted any of the money from the sale, they would have to help her. Of course Delilah was in charge of handling all of the money during the sale, and after she took what she believed she deserved, Joey and Steven were left with very little. Soon after, the house was put for sale and sold. Clara's second car was also sold. Delilah declared the only assets Joey and Steven were entitled to was their portion of the money made selling the house and car. These assets also included the sale of Clara's mobile home, which happened to have been sold to Mike.

Before distributing the money to anyone, she used that money to pay all of Clara's debts, including her funeral costs and the cost to have her husband's body exhumed and moved to the cemetery in Johnston to lie next to Clara. Delilah had two large marble slabs placed on top of John and Clara's graves. She told Beth that Clara's will specified slabs be placed on top of the graves, however, when Beth reviewed the will, there was no mention of marble slabs. Beth wondered why Delilah had done this.

In the end, Joey and Steven each received approximately twenty thousand dollars, while Delilah estimated that she and Mike got seven hundred thousand dollars, despite the fact that Clara's will stated Mike was to receive one half of her estate, while Joey and Steven were each to receive one quarter.

Louise told Beth, "I told your mother that Aunt Clara said she wanted to make sure that Joey and Steven knew how much money she had. She told Joey she had four accounts at the bank and that your father's name was on all of them, in case he needed money to pay for her care."

"I didn't know that she had so many accounts. My father did tell me that my mother forced Aunt Clara to include my father's name on her accounts, but I didn't know how many accounts she had. What was my mother's reaction?"

"She got very upset. She told me it was none of my business."

"But it is your business. Did Joey talk to her?"

"Yeah, she told him he'll get what she decides to give him."

"But the will states he should get one quarter of the entire estate."

Louise exhaled as she shook her head. "Yeah, but your mother will decide what's included in the estate. Beth, have you ever discussed this with Steven?"

"Yeah, Steven doesn't care. He says he'll be happy if he gets anything at all. He never expected anything. He assumed Clara would leave her money to her mother, sister, and brother. Have you or Joey spoken to the attorney?"

Louise threw up her arms. "He told Joey that everything that was done, was done with Clara's consent. When Joey asked for proof, the attorney told him his word was proof enough. He won't be of any help, except to your mother."

"Unless you or Joey can get a look at Aunt Clara's bank records, I think you're out of luck."

"Typical, when dealing with your mother."

א

A few days later Blanche, one of Beth's aunts, invited her out to lunch. When Beth arrived at the restaurant, she noticed Delilah there. Beth's jaw dropped and her eyes widened. As she sat down, she noticed her aunt had one side of her mouth raised and she was shaking her head.

"Mom, I didn't expect you to be here."

"I was on my way to shop for some new furniture. I drove past Blanche's house and noticed her car pulling away. Since it was close to lunchtime, I assumed she was going out to eat and I followed her here. What a surprise to see you here; you didn't tell me about this."

"I guess we're both surprised."

Delilah reached into her purse and pulled out four bank books. "I had to open four separate accounts. The stupid ass bank will only insure each account for two hundred thousand dollars. How stupid. I've decided, now that I have all of this money, I'm buying new furniture and I'm having drapes custom-made. I'm going to buy whatever I want. Beth, do you want new furniture?"

"No, my furniture is fine."

"Oh yeah, that's right, you're the big shot with new furniture."

Beth looked at her aunt. They both rolled their eyes.

"Should we order now?" Beth asked, not wanting to talk to her mother about this any longer.

"Yes, let's," Blanche answered.

Delilah added, "Yes, let's, I have shopping to do."

They ordered and ate their lunch in silence, Beth and her aunt both disgusted by Delilah's presence. As they left the restaurant, Beth gave her Aunt Blanche a hug. "Thanks for the invite. We'll have to try this again sometime."

"We'll try," her aunt responded, throwing a glance at Delilah.

Delilah looked at Beth. "Do you want to come shopping with me? We can go anywhere. Do you want some new clothes or jewelry?"

"No thanks, Mom, I have to get home. I have to pick Joseph up at school. See you soon."

As Beth turned to leave, she heard Delilah say, "But I can buy you anything you want."

"No thanks, Mom. Goodbye."

As she drove away, Beth noticed Delilah getting into Aunt Clara's collector car.

א

A few days later, Louise phoned Beth.

"I don't understand your mother; she kicks me out of her house into the cold, dark night, endangering our lives, but still calls for help and to complain. Joey helped out with Aunt Clara's estate, but now that it's final, he wants nothing to do with your mother. It breaks his heart because it means he will be estranged from your dad. Maybe if you can ever get your dad alone, you can let him know Joey would like to get together. The two of them can meet without your mother around."

"It's unfortunate. With both of their parents and Uncle Paul gone, they only have each other."

"That's what breaks Joey's heart."

"I can imagine."

"Well, your mother called me yesterday to complain about you. She said you met with her and your aunt for lunch. Neither of you told her you were meeting. She said she asked you to go shopping but you refused. I think she is mad that she can't buy you. I have to tell you, Beth, I think she sees you as a threat."

Louise hesitated before she continued. "She said, once your dad is dead, she'll call social services and claim you abuse your children. She is hoping you'll go to jail and she'll get custody of your kids."

"That's laughable. Everyone, including my children, knows they are not abused. Plus, my children do have a father who is capable of maintaining custody," Beth said, hoping she was right. "She needs help."

"Or jail time."

"Yeah or jail time. She sees me as a threat because she tells me everything. I'm the one who knows who she truly is. She makes threats because she thinks it will prevent me from acting on what I know. If she worries about me saying something to someone, why does she tell me everything? I just don't get it."

"I don't know."

As Beth hung up the phone, she said a silent prayer. *Now that she has everything she wanted: her freedom from Helen, revenge on Margaret, and wealth from Clara; I hope this nightmare will end.*

Chapter 21

B eth knew she had to do something about her mother but decided she would talk to Edward before doing anything. He was always levelheaded and analyzed pros and cons of everything before taking action. Beth knew if Edward agreed with her, she must take action.

Beth paced through her house all afternoon, unable to eat or sit still. She was anxious to talk to Edward. *Will he share my fear?* Beth feared that Delilah did the unimaginable; that she would try to take Beth's children away; that nobody would listen, leaving Delilah free to murder again.

That became the longest afternoon of Beth's life. She was glad Joseph was with her. His boyish antics helped to keep her mind temporarily off Delilah.

When Beth put Joseph down for a nap, she watched him close his eyes and drift off to sleep. Then it hit her and she began to cry. *Would Delilah be able to take her boys away? Would anyone believe her? Social services believed Delilah in the past, would they believe her again?*

Beth knew she could lose her children, but she couldn't sit by and do nothing.

"Edward, please be home on time," she whispered through her sobs.

Joseph woke up from his nap and came running down the hall. He ran to Beth and wrapped his chubby arms around her legs. "I love you, Mommy."

"I love you too, sweetie."

Beth bent down and held him tight, trying in vain to hold back the tears. He returned Beth's hug and melted her heart.

Just then Beth's other two sons came bursting through the door, home from school, anxious to share their day. They gave Beth a hug and ran into the kitchen, where there were usually homemade cookies warm from the oven waiting for them. Beth learned this habit from her Grandma Helen when she was a little girl. Today there were no cookies. Realizing her boys needed her helped; Beth overcame her sadness and sifted through her kitchen cabinets to find some crackers and peanut butter. She made some hot chocolate and gave her boys their afternoon snack.

They all sat around the kitchen table, the boys telling Beth about their day. She smiled at the sight. She loved her boys, and they loved her. They were so happy. Beth was certain social services would see that. Delilah couldn't take them away.

Beth was glad when Edward finally came through the door. As he got to the top of the stairs, all three boys left their chairs and ran to him giving him hugs. "I missed you, Daddy," Joseph said.

"I missed you too, and I missed Mommy. Where is Mommy?"

Beth walked through the kitchen door, into Edward's waiting arms. Edward felt her melt into him. He bent down and kissed her wet cheek. "What's wrong? Are you okay?"

Beth wiped her eyes with her sleeve, straightening herself up. "Wait until the boys are gone," she whispered.

Beth instructed the boys to wash their hands and faces before dinner. When they were gone she turned back to Edward. "Do you think my mother is capable of murder?"

Edward took a step back, his face turned ashen. "I didn't want to upset you, but I've thought that same thing. Yes, I do."

The boys returned and as they ate dinner, Beth and Edward would sneak glances at each other, noticing the sorrow in each other's eyes. Beth was glad the boys were too wrapped up in their own worlds to notice that their parents were upset.

After dinner Edward helped the boys finish their homework while Beth cleaned up. When they were finished, Beth told the boys to take their baths and get ready for bed. She read each of them a story as they drifted off to sleep. As they each began to drift, she kissed them on their cheeks and said, "I love you. Have sweet dreams." Beth wished she had heard those words from her own mother, but she could not remember Delilah ever saying "I love you."

Beth found Edward downstairs in the family room.

"You know, sweetheart, I thought it was strange that both of your grandmothers and Aunt Clara were told by their doctors that they were healthy and should expect to live a long life only to die a few weeks later while with your mother. I realize that it is possible, but three people within less than three years...that does not seem like a co-incidence. I have doubts, and I didn't want to upset you, but I knew you would do the right thing."

"It's difficult for me to believe, but I agree. I'm just so afraid. My mother keeps threatening to take the children away, and social services can't seem to see through her. They think she's a really nice person. I'm afraid they will believe her and not believe me."

"Sweetheart, I'm behind you one hundred percent. I don't believe she can take our children. You are a wonderful mother and our children are happy. They love you. I won't let her take our children."

"But what if nobody believes me? What if people keep dying when they're with her? Do you know that Aunt Katherine called and said she would go live with my mother when she's ready to die? She said that everyone who lives with Delilah dies."

Beth put her head in her hands. "I don't know what to do. I believe you will fight for our children, but you know she has a way of charming people. If she takes our boys away, I'm afraid they will suffer the same fate as my grandmothers and Aunt Clara. I won't let that happen."

"She only threatens you so you will be afraid and not say anything. I believe she is more afraid of you than you are of her. She's afraid you will report your suspicions and she'll spend the rest of her life in jail. Boy, would that be horrible for her. She would not be able to spend all of Clara's money; she would not be able to control every-thing. No honey, I don't believe she will do anything. She is afraid of you. Only you know the truth."

Edward took hold of Beth's hand. "Beth, you know I love you, right? And I'll do everything I can to protect our boys."

"I know, and I'm grateful," Beth said, giving Ed-ward's hand a squeeze, "but my mother still scares me. I don't know what to do. I don't know who to trust."

Beth looked pleadingly into her husband's eyes. "What should I do?"

"You should try to get a good night sleep. The boys

will be up early. Sleep on it. In the morning, talk to your Aunt Louise and Uncle Joey. Find out how they feel. I think you can trust them. Together the four of us will figure it out."

"You're right. I can trust Joey and Louise. After all, Joey lost his mother and aunt. He will want to see justice served. Thank you for helping me think it through and for offering your opinion."

Beth put her hand on Edward's cheek. "I'm so thankful to have you in my life, loving me and our children. I love you."

"It's my pleasure, sweetheart. I love you too. Now let's go to bed and try to sleep. Try to clear your mind. You need to sleep to conserve your strength. You've had a couple of hard, very emotional days and now you have some hard decisions to make. You need a clear head to make those decisions."

"Thank you for your love and support," Beth said giving her husband a soft kiss on the lips. "I'll call Louise and Joey in the morning."

Chapter 22

"Hi, Louise, it's Beth."

"Hi, Beth, I was just thinking about you. How is Jack? Cooper has been really upset. He keeps asking why your mother made us leave when it was so cold and dark. He said he never saw anyone so angry. Her screaming and profanity really scared him. When I put him to bed last night, he said he never wants to sleep in a car again, it was so dark and he was so cold. And Joey is distraught. I'm not sure if he is more upset that Aunt Clara died or that your mother is a lunatic. I don't know how to help him."

"I'm sorry, Louise. Jack was pretty upset too. He has never seen such violence. He would not leave my side while we were at Aunt Clara's house. He was afraid of being hit by some flying object. He asked me why Grandma was so angry. He asked if Grandma would hurt him. I'm angry with her but I'm more afraid for my dad. I wish I could convince him to leave, but I know he never will."

"I know what you mean. Joey and I were talking about the way your mother abused both of your grandmothers, and we're also afraid for your father. He is the only one close to her now. Beth, we are so afraid for him."

"Thanks for your concern. All we can do is talk to him and keep our eyes open."

"Beth, Joey and I cannot help you with your dad. Joey never wants to see your mother again, but maybe if you can get your dad alone, without your mother, Joey can talk to him."

"That's the way it's been my entire life. Everyone becomes angry with her and stays away, or they're just too afraid of her to help me do anything. I've been fighting the Delilah battle alone my whole life. Speaking of my dad and being afraid, Edward and I had a long conversation last night. We both wonder if my mother might be directly responsible for the deaths of Aunt Clara and both of my grandmothers."

Beth heard a large gasp on the other end of the telephone, then she heard Louise began to sob.

"Louise, what's wrong?"

"Oh Beth, Joey and I had the same conversation. I just didn't know how to tell you. What are we going to do?"

"I don't know. Maybe I can call Edward's friend Rob Horne and ask his opinion. Remember, Rob is a

Chicago police officer?"

"That's right. I forgot about that. I think that's a great place to start. What can I do to help?"

"All I need is your support, Louise. I'll do the rest. I don't want Delilah getting mad at anyone but me. Did I tell you that Aunt Katherine called me?"

"No, when did she call? She never calls anyone."

"Two days ago. She called to tell me she will go to live with my mother when she is ready to die since that's what happens to everyone that lives with my mother."

"Oh my gosh, Beth, did she really say that?"

"Yes, that's what scared me into believing it might be true, and I have to do something."

"Wait till Joey hears that. He won't believe it. Have you told anyone else?"

"Only Edward. He agrees that we have to do something. I'm going to call Rob right now"

"Let me know if I can help in any way," Louise said.

"I will, thanks."

Beth hung up the phone and called the Chicago police department, district two, and asked for Rob Horne. She was happy to hear that he was in the station that day.

"Hi Beth, what's up? How's Edward?"

"Edward's fine but I'm not. I have a concern I would like to discuss with you. Can we meet somewhere?"

"Sure, cook me dinner and I'll be over right after work. Will Edward be home?"

Rob realized if Beth needed to share her concern,

it must be important. Rob admired Beth for her high integrity.

"Yeah, he'll be here. Can Cheryl come along with you?"

"Sure, I'll call her right now so she won't start dinner."

"Okay, I'll see you both at six."

"Okay, see you then."

Edward and Rob had been friends since childhood. They became such good friends that Edward asked Rob to be best man at their wedding. By the time Beth met Rob, he was already dating Cheryl. They all took an instant liking to each other and became inseparable friends. Rob and Cheryl married only six months after Edward and Beth.

Beth fed the children early. They were in their bedrooms doing their homework when Rob and Cheryl arrived.

Cheryl gave Beth a hug. "What's wrong? You're shaking."

Rob glanced at Beth. "Beth, what's wrong?" He turned to look at Edward, who had a look of anguish on his face. "Ed, buddy, what's going on?"

Beth started up the stairs. "Let's sit down. We'll talk during dinner."

"Okay, but you better start talking soon; you are both worrying me."

As they all sat down to dinner, Beth began.

"Rob, both of my grandmothers and my dad's aunt died within thirty-two months of each other, and they all

193

died of heart failure while in my parents' home. One died in Maple Grass, Illinois; two died in Johnston, Wisconsin. Rob, I'm scared, I don't know what to do. I've called social services numerous times and police were called once. They all say there is nothing they can do. Rob, what can I do? Am I just crazy? My mother threatens to take the children away if I say or do anything. I'm afraid she will try to follow up on her threat if I share my concern about her. Oh, Rob, what should I do?"

Cheryl dropped her fork. "Holy crap, Beth!"

"I agree Beth. Holy crap. In all of my years on the force, I have never heard anything so horrifying. Why didn't you say something sooner?"

"I didn't want to burden you. Since the police and social services had told me there was nothing I could do, I believed there was nothing that could be done. And I'm so scared."

"I understand. Let me look into it. Which PD did you call? I'll try to get their report in the morning."

"A neighbor of my parents called Maple Grass PD three summers ago when they heard my mother abusing my father. My father would not press charges so it was dropped."

"I'll call them in the morning. Do you have a report number or the officer's name?"

"No, I never asked. I guess I should have, but I don't know if my father would have had that information.

I'm sure my mother would have destroyed anything."

"Beth, I'm so sorry."

"Thanks, Rob."

When Beth was ready to serve dessert, she brought the boys out of their rooms so they could join in. After dessert, Rob, Cheryl, and Edward sat watching TV while Beth put the boys to bed.

When Beth returned, Cheryl rose and gave Beth a hug. "I'm here for you. Whatever you need. Boy, this is heavy. I can't believe you carried this inside without sharing it with anyone. It must have really eaten at you."

"You have no idea. I'm glad I had Edward." Beth squeezed Cheryl's hand. "Thanks for your support. You both are the best."

"After I call Maple Grass PD, I'll talk to my Sergeant and try to put together a plan of action. Have you thought about hiring a PI?" Rob asked.

"No, why should I hire a PI?"

"There are so many jurisdictions to deal with here, that it might be quicker for them to get information. Our department has used several good PI's. I'll get you their numbers."

"Thanks. I'll call my Uncle Joey and Aunt Louise in the morning to get their opinion."

"Beth, you look exhausted. We're going to leave. You did the right thing to call me. There's nothing else you can do tonight. Get some sleep. Police orders," Rob said with a warm smile.

"I'll try. Thank you both. I'll be anxious for your call tomorrow."

The couples stood and Beth and Edward escorted them to the door.

"Good night, Beth. Thanks for delicious dinner. Call me if you need anything. I mean it."

"Thanks, Cheryl, I will."

"Me too. I'll call you in the morning after I contact Maple Grass PD and talk to my sergeant. Sleep well. Take care of her, Edward. See you pal."

"Night, Rob. Thanks for coming."

Chapter 23

After a fitful, sleepless night, Beth garnered enough energy to get Edward and the children ready for their day and off to work and school.

She sat quietly at her kitchen table thinking about the conversation she had with Rob. She was anxious for his call. She hoped he would provide some guidance.

As she was contemplating whether to call Aunt Louise now or wait until after Rob's call, the telephone rang. She brought the phone to her ear, expecting it to be Rob.

"Hi, Beth. Are you up and dressed?"

"Hi, Mom. I'm up but I'm not dressed."

"You know, Beth, isn't it strange that Aunt Clara and both grandmas died while they were with me? You know I took really good care of all of them. I didn't do anything wrong. I would never hurt or kill anyone. You know that right?"

Beth's knees buckled and she had to sit back down. "Where did that come from?"

"I was just thinking it might look suspicious. I asked the coroner when he came out for Aunt Clara if anything looked suspicious, but he didn't answer. Do you think it looked suspicious?"

"I don't know, Mom, I wasn't there. I gotta go," Beth said hastily. With what was going on, she didn't feel comfortable talking to her mother at that moment. As Beth was hanging up the phone, she heard Delilah in the background, "I never killed anyone."

Beth started to shake, her chest heaved and tears fell fast and heavy. *She did do it!* she thought to herself. *I have to do something.*

Beth stood there shaking. She felt numb, when the phone rang again. *Please don't let it be her.*

"Hi Beth, its Rob. How's it going?"

"Rob, I'm glad you called." Her voice trembled. "Any word from Maple Grass?"

"Beth, what's wrong?" Rob asked, sensing the fear in her voice. "You sound scared."

"I am scared. My mother just called. It was eerie. She kept saying she never killed anyone."

Beth had to sit down again.

"That is scary. Why would she say that if she wasn't thinking it? You know Beth, my years of experience have taught me, it's usually the guilty that work the hardest to prove their innocence. You better be careful."

"I'm trying to be," she said, taking a deep breath. "What about Maple Grass?"

"Bad news, you are right. Since your father would not press charges, the case was closed. The only way to reopen the case would be for someone to witness your mother abusing your father and report it. But if your father is still unwilling to press charges, there is nothing anyone can do. I spoke to one of the officers that went to your parents' home. He believed your mother was abusing your father and probably your grandmother too. He feels she is a menace to society, however, unless anyone presses charges or they witness it themselves, there's nothing they can do." Beth sighed as Rob continued, "I wish I had better news. I'm afraid I won't be able to help you right now. If something changes, I'll let you know. If you receive any additional information, let me know. I'm so sorry, Beth. I wish I could've done something."

"You know Rob, I have a taped conversation I had with my mother. In it she admits to slapping my grandmother, and putting her on the porch while soaking wet, in the middle of winter. Surely, we can use that against her."

"I'm afraid we would get the same response I got when I called Maple Grass, asking about the time your mother abused your father. If the conversation was not witnessed by social services or the P.D., it is not admissible in a court of law. I'm afraid we won't be able to use that either."

"Thanks for trying Rob. This is what I have been up against my whole life. Unless it's witnessed, it hasn't happened. It's so frustrating."

"It's frustrating for us too. We know people are guilty but without evidence or a direct witness, there is nothing we can do. Everyone I talk to about your case believes your mother was directly involved with all three deaths, however, our hands are tied. Again, Beth, I'm so sorry."

Beth sighed a little louder. "Rob, if you think of anything else that I can do, please let me know."

"I mailed you a list of some of the private investigators our department uses. You should have it in the mail tomorrow. Maybe you could try calling the feds. Since Delilah had bodies transported across state lines, they may be interested, but many people transport family members across state lines for burial. I don't have much hope, but you can try. You can also try to call the IRS. If she didn't report the cash she found, they can get her on tax evasion, but again, how can you prove it? If she deposited a large sum of money in her bank account that's unaccounted for and there's no evidence, she will just deny it. You're in a tough position. You've come toe to toe with a real pro. Other than contacting the private investigator, you have done everything you can and then some. You know Beth, most people who were shot down as much as you would have given up. I admire your determination. I'll keep on this case to see if I can get something to break. You hang in there."

"Thanks, Rob."

"You're welcome. Keep your chin up."

Beth got up from her chair, walked over and hung up the phone, still feeling numb. She walked to the stove and made herself a cup of tea. She sat back down at the table, cupped her head in her hands, and cried.

After about five minutes, she was able to compose herself. She stood up and reached for the phone, sat back down, took a sip of tea and dialed. When Beth heard her Aunt Louise answer on the other end, her sobs began again.

"Hi, Louise, I did call Rob Horne as we discussed. He just called me back."

Beth sniffled, trying to hold back her tears. "We're up against a brick wall. He suggested we hire a private investigator. Maybe they will be able to dig deeper and uncover something. He said there is nothing the police department can do. He even spoke to Maple Grass about the time they went to my parents' house."

"Louise, I'm so afraid," she said through her tears. "I don't know what to do. Rob thinks my mother was involved, but at this time he can't help."

"We'll think of something. At least Rob believes us. That's more than social services did. Maybe we should get a private investigator involved. I'll talk to Joey when he gets home. What does Edward think?"

"I haven't spoken to him yet. He is supportive of whatever we decide to do. He believes something must be done."

"I'm so sorry for you, Beth. You are carrying the heaviest part of this burden. Your mother is evil."

"She is who she is. You and I can't change her. She will only be changed if she sits in jail for the rest of her life."

"If only we could make that happen."

"If only," Beth replied.

After ending her conversation with Louise, Beth found her Yellow Pages and sat back down at the kitchen table. She thumbed through, looking for private investigators as she finished her tea. Although she knew Rob Horne had mailed her information, she couldn't wait to begin to contact someone.

The first person she contacted happened to have been an ex-FBI agent. Beth was excited; Rob suggested she contact the FBI. Maybe this person could help. The agent listened intently. He then proceeded to tell Beth that he agreed that these deaths looked suspicious; however, without hard evidence there was nothing he could do. He also said that it was common for bodies to be transported to another state for burial. He suggested Beth contact law enforcement agencies in the town these women died. He felt they may be able to uncover information that an investigator may not, since each agency had a different system. He also suggested that she contact each state's Department of Criminal Investigation. He explained that the criminal investigation departments would be able to collaborate.

Beth thanked him for his time and opinion, hung up the phone, sat at the kitchen table and cried.

Will anyone be able to help me stop my mother?

Chapter 24

That day happened to be Joseph's first day of preschool. He was excited as he declared he was now a big boy like his brothers. Beth struggled to pull herself back together after her conversation with the ex-FBI investigator. She decided to walk the one and a half blocks to the preschool to pick up Joseph versus driving there.

When she arrived, Joseph came running to her. "Mommy, I had fun, but I'm not coming back here."

"Why not?"

"I miss you."

Beth looked at his teachers. Both had great big smiles as they looked at Joseph. As she approached, the teacher said, "He is such a pleasure. He's a wonderful child, but he misses his mommy. You sure are loved."

Beth's heart pounded with delight. "Thanks, I needed to hear that. He sure is loved."

"We can tell. Have a good afternoon. We'll see you and Joseph on Wednesday."

All the way home Joseph told Beth what he had learned that day, all the fun he had with his new friends, but he still remained adamant about not returning. Beth was filled with joy that Joseph loved her so much and that he had such a good time and felt free to express himself. Her bubble quickly burst when she remembered her early school days, walking to and from school with Delilah.

Beth suffered constant ridicule. Nothing she did was ever good enough for her mother. Delilah would pick out Beth's clothes, then tell her how stupid her outfit looked. She combed Beth's hair, then halfway to school she would pull Beth's hair and tell her she didn't like the way it was combed. Beth remembered crying all the way to school some mornings, because after she was dressed, Delilah would change her mind and decide Beth should wear something different. She would lay the new outfit out on Beth's bed while Beth was busy washing her face and brushing her teeth so she wouldn't notice. As she walked out of the bathroom, Delilah would take the belt out of the kitchen drawer and beat her for not changing her outfit. Delilah told Beth she must always be perfect; if she were not, people would think Delilah was not a perfect mother. Beth vowed never to treat her children so horribly.

Beth delighted in her time with Joseph, as she did with Jon and Jack. They helped her temporarily forget about Delilah.

Beth fed Joseph lunch, then put him down for his nap. She went into the living room and sat on the sofa, looking out the picture window, watching the snow that had begun to fall. She loved the gentle glow of the gaslight in front of her house and thought the snowflakes seem to sparkle in that glow. She sat wondering what her next move should be.

As she was watching out the window, she saw the mailman turn into her driveway, walk up the sidewalk and up the stairs. She heard him close the mailbox that was attached to the house. She went outside and retrieved the mail. As she thumbed through the pile, she noticed an envelope from the Chicago Police Department. She opened it to find the list of private investigators Rob had promised. It arrived sooner than she expected.

"Maybe one of these people can help me," she said with excitement.

She looked down the list of names with their bios, until she came to one that seemed to stick out: Laura Nelson, private investigator. Her biography indicated that she had been on the Chicago police force for twenty years. She retired five years previously and set up her own private investigation office. It also indicated she had worked with the state's attorney to apprehend a criminal from the FBI's most wanted list. Even though the first PI she had talked to couldn't help her, Beth hoped that since Laura was able to apprehend a dangerous wanted criminal, she would be able to help her convict Delilah.

She stood up and walked to the kitchen. She picked up the phone and called her Aunt Louise.

"Hi Louise, I received that list of private investigators from Rob. One woman, Laura Nelson, sounds very interesting. I have the feeling she may be able to help. I'll call Rob at home tonight and ask if he knows her personally." Beth exhaled. "I have to do this. I hope Joey agrees, but if he doesn't, I'll do it on my own. I can't sit and do nothing. I'm sure Edward will agree with me. He has already told me something must be done."

"I'm sure Joey will agree too. Oh, Beth, I hope this is the answer we have been looking for."

"I hope so too. I'm just concerned that my mother will find out and try to make good on her promise to take my children away. I'm also concerned for my father. I sure hope she doesn't do anything to him."

"I hope not too. I don't know what your mother is capable of anymore. She seems to get more brazen after each death."

"I agree. It seems the more she gets away with, the more empowered she becomes. I'll call Laura in the morning. Can you talk to Joey tonight?"

"Yes, I'll talk to him as soon as he gets home. Call me after you've talked to Laura."

"Okay, I will. I'll talk to you tomorrow."

As Beth hung up the phone, her heart began to

pound with excitement. *Maybe we can stop her!*

Beth was giddy as she began to compile ingredients to make cookies. Joseph heard the commotion and woke from his nap. He entered the kitchen, "Yay, it's time to make cookies! I'll help."

Beth bent down and gave him a big hug and kiss on the cheek.

"Yuck," he said as he wiped his cheek with his sleeve.

Before the cookies were finished baking, the front door burst open and Jon and Jack ran inside.

Jack screeched, "Yum, chocolate chip," as he ran up the stairs.

Beth stepped into the hallway. "One minute, Mister. Off with those boots."

The three boys sat down around the kitchen table as Beth poured their milk. She took the cookies from the oven and put them on a plate. Beth felt happy and content as she watched her boys. She remembered coming home from school, sometimes to an empty home, sometimes to Delilah ignoring her because she was on the telephone or, on several occasions, to see a strange man leaving out the back door as Beth was walking in the front, never knowing who these men were.

The boys finished their snacks and ran off to do homework or read books as Beth cooked dinner. Edward returned home from work, and they all ate dinner. After they were done, Beth cleaned the kitchen while Edward helped the boys finish their homework and then tucked them into bed.

When she was finished cleaning, Beth went downstairs. Edward was in the family room watching the news. She curled up next to him on the sofa and laid her head on his chest. He put his arm around her and gently caressed her hair. Beth told Edward about her conversation with Rob Horne and about the list of private investigators Rob sent her.

"One person, Laura Nelson, looks like someone who may be able to help me. I'd like to ask Rob about her, and if he agrees, I'd like to hire her."

"Have you talked this over with Joey?"

"No, but I discussed it with Louise. She will talk to Joey tonight."

"Well, it's okay with me, wait and see what Joey thinks."

"I'd like to call Rob tonight to get his opinion, that way I'll be ready to talk to Joey."

"Sure, give them a call now."

She kissed his cheek. "Thanks for your support."

Beth went upstairs to call Rob. Cheryl answered.

"Hi, Beth, how are you? I've been thinking about you so much since our visit. I wanted to call you, but I didn't know if you wanted to talk."

"I'm doing okay. I have my moments, but the children keep me busy, and I've been trying to decide what to do. I've been talking to Rob and he's been a lot of help."

"Rob told me. We both feel so bad. We wish there

was something we could do for you."

"Just be there. That's what I need. Speaking of Rob, is he home?"

"He is chomping at the bit to talk to you. Take care, Beth. Call me if you need me."

"Thanks, Cheryl. I will."

Rob came to the phone.

"Hey, what's up? Do you have anything new?"

"No, but I did get that list you mailed me."

"Wow, that was fast."

"Yeah, I reviewed it and one person stood out to me. Do you know Laura Nelson?"

"Know her," Rob chuckled, "she was my partner for two years, until she retired. We always kid each other that she retired because of working with me. She's a great investigator and a good person. I think you would like her. She would do a good job for you."

Beth exhaled. "Thanks, Rob. It's hard to decide to hire someone without knowing anything about them. You made me feel so much better."

"When did you plan on calling her?"

"Tomorrow morning."

"Great, I'll call her tonight to fill her in. Good luck, Beth. Let me know if I can do anything else."

"Thanks, Rob. You've done a lot. Tell Cheryl good-bye for me."

"Will do. Say hi to Edward."

"I will."

Beth hung up the phone and went back downstairs to sit with Edward. As she entered the family room, he looked up at her.

"You look more relaxed. I assume your conversation with Rob went well."

"Yes, it did. Laura Nelson was his partner for two years. He recommended her highly. He said he will call her tonight, and I will call her in the morning. Oh, by the way Rob said hi."

As Beth sat down next to Edward, he put his arm around her and kissed her on her forehead. "I'm glad you're feeling better. I don't like seeing you sad."

She leaned her head on his shoulder, feeling secure in his love and hopeful for the first time in a long time.

Chapter 25

Beth was surprised when the doorbell rang the next morning. *Please don't let it be my mother.*

She opened the front door.

"What a surprise. I never would've expected you, especially this early."

"Joey wanted me to be here first thing this morning," Louise said. "He wants to be sure you have support when you call the investigator."

"So I assume the two of you talked it over."

"Yeah, Joey agrees, we have to try to do something. Have you spoken to Edward?"

"He's in total agreement."

"Good, let's get some coffee and call."

Beth and Louise walked upstairs into the kitchen. Louise sat down on a chair while Beth brewed a pot of coffee. Beth left the kitchen, returning a few minutes later with the box of Kleenex, two pads of paper, and two pencils, which she set on the kitchen table. She poured two cups of coffee, set them on the table, grabbed the telephone, and sat down. She felt her heart pounding and began shaking. She turned and looked at Louise.

"Are you ready? Here goes nothing."

Louise reached across the table to grab Beth's hand. "Let's do this."

Beth's hands were shaking as she dialed the phone.

"Hello, Nelson private investigations, Laura speaking."

Beth's voice quivered. "Hello Laura, my name is Bethany Jasdam. A mutual friend, Rob Horne, suggested I give you a call."

"Son of a gun, how is Rob? We were partners on the police force."

"Yeah, he told me. He and Cheryl are both doing fine. Didn't Rob call you? He said he would."

"He may have tried; I've been on a case and un-available until this morning. I'm glad Rob and Cheryl are doing well. How can I help you?"

Through her tears Beth relayed her story, glancing at Louise for reassurance every now and again. Laura listened without interrupting, until Beth had finished.

"Wow, that's some story. I would love to try to help you. Do you feel that you may be in danger? It sounds like your mother will stop at nothing to get what she wants."

"I am afraid; however, I'm more afraid of doing

213

nothing. I've had a lengthy conversation with my husband and my aunt and uncle. They are all supportive of me and will work together to try to keep me safe. My biggest fears are my mother's threat to take away my children and what she might do to my father."

"I don't see how she could take away your children, Beth"

"I don't think she could either, but if she tried, it would be very difficult for them."

"I don't think you have anything to worry about. I will keep the investigation confidential. I will only interview people that you can trust not to tell her. We'll keep your children and your father safe."

"Thank you for the reassurance," Beth said. "When can we meet?"

"How about Thursday? There is a restaurant, Five Stars, on the corner of Archer and Narragansett. We can meet for lunch. How does that sound?"

"That works for me."

"Before we meet, I'd like you to contact your local police criminal investigator. I want them to know what's going on. I need their help to keep you safe."

"Okay, if you insist, I'll call them."

"Good, I'll see you Thursday. I have short brown, curly hair, and I'll have a brown briefcase. I meet clients at Five Stars often, so if you don't recognize me, ask the hostess. I'll be there a little early, around eleven forty-five, so I won't miss you. It's been great talking to you.

Oh, Beth, would you mind if I collaborate with Rob? I'd like his input."

"No, I don't mind. He's been a big help already and he's a good friend. I'm sure he would like to help if he could. See you Thursday."

Beth stood up, hung up the phone, and fell back into her chair. She exhaled and looked at Louise.

"What a relief. Maybe we can finally get help."

"I hope so. Beth, would you mind if Joey and I met Laura with you? Joey said since you are handling all of the emotional aspects of the investigation, he would like to handle the financial side. He will want to meet Laura and pay her on Thursday."

"That would be great. I could use the support. I don't expect you to pay for the investigation. Maybe we can share the expense."

"No, Joey has put aside some money from Clara's estate just for this purpose."

"If you and Joey insist."

"We do." Louise stood and stepped towards Beth, bending down to give Beth a hug. "I tried to protect both of your grandmothers but I couldn't. At least we can pay for the investigation that hopefully will send your mother to jail."

"I hope so."

They finished their coffee and Louise left. Beth picked up her local Yellow Pages and looked up the police department's criminal investigation number.

"Sergeant Dace."

"Hi, Sergeant, my name is Bethany Jasdam. I'm working with private investigator Laura Nelson. She suggested I call your office and explain my case. She is worried about my safety and hopes you can help."

"I'll sure try. I've worked with Laura before. She was with the Police Department. She's a good person. I think she'll be thorough. And she's fair but tough."

"All the attributes my case requires."

Sergeant Dace chuckled. "So, tell me what's going on."

Here we go again, Beth thought.

Beth relayed her story with a heavy heart. When she finished, Sergeant Dace replied, "It *does* sound like you need protection. My experience has shown that people who abuse their own mothers, won't stop at anything. They remove any obstacle in their way. Where do your children attend school? Can I have your permission to contact their school?"

"I don't think she would hurt my children, but sure, you can talk to school."

"I wouldn't put anything past her. She may not physically abuse them, but she may mentally abuse them, trying to alienate their affection from you. I would like to meet and have you sign a release for the school. Are you busy now? Can I come over?"

"Sure."

"Okay. See you in ten minutes."

Beth hung up the phone, took a deep breath, and started to cry.

When the doorbell rang, she dried her eyes and walked down the stairs to open the door. In front of her stood a middle-aged man, about five feet eight inches tall with a medium build. He wore a dark suit in need of a good pressing and an ivory-colored shirt and green tie. He pulled back the corner of his suit jacket to reveal his police badge.

"Hi, Beth, I'm Sergeant Dace."

"Nice to meet you. Please come in."

He stepped in and gave a quick look around. "Beautiful home. It still smells like Christmas."

"Thank you. Yes, I spray pine tree-scented air freshener until February. I hate giving up Christmas. Would you like something to drink?"

"No thanks. Where should we sit?"

Beth led him up the stairs and into the living room where he sat on the sofa. Beth sat in the club chair.

"The first thing I want to do is visit your childrens' school. I'll make sure they will only be released to you or your husband. In an emergency you can call me to authorize someone else. No one will be allowed access to your children while they are in school. I will ask that they be monitored on the playground and we'll have a car driving around before and after school."

"Is all of this really necessary? My children will be

uncomfortable."

"They won't know we're there. They'll think we're just doing our jobs protecting everyone. Yes, I do think it's necessary. As I said on the phone, someone who would harm their own mother is capable of anything, especially considering all the threats that she has made. Now, how can I protect you?"

"I don't think I need protection. My mother has never threatened me, just my children."

Beth noticed Sergeant Dace wrinkle his brow. "I'm afraid of what her reaction might be if she finds out she's being investigated. I'll talk to Laura, if it's okay with you. I'll ask her not to tell anyone that you initiated the investigation. Laura's right to be concerned for your safety. I'll make sure I have a car go by your home every half-hour. What kind of car does your mother drive?

"She has a classic gold Cadillac."

"That should be easy to spot. I'll add that to my notes," he said, jotting the information in a small notepad.

Then he reached in his satchel, pulled out some papers, and set them on the coffee table. "Here are the release forms I need you to sign. One for school, one for Laura." He pulled out a business card and a pen. "Here's my card with my phone number. Keep it with you at all times." Before handing the card to Beth, he wrote something on the back. "I've included my pager number. Contact me day or night."

"Thank you, Sergeant Dace. I do feel safer now.

Mostly I need to keep my boys safe."

Beth got an inquisitive look on her face. "Do you think she would hurt my husband, or Joey and Louise and their family?"

"She did threaten Louise's children. I wouldn't put anything past her. Tell them to keep their eyes and ears open. They should call their local department and have a detail on their kids, probably on both of them too. Beth, from what you've said, I do believe she was involved in all three deaths. It is unlikely these women just happened to die of heart failure while with your mother, especially since they also had other living arrangements. Your mother certainly had motive and assured herself the opportunity. I have no doubt in my mind. Now, we just need to prove it."

Beth signed the releases and handed them back to Sergeant Dace.

"Thank you for everything."

"I'll go to school as soon as I leave here. I'll call when I get back to my office and let you know if anything changes or if I receive any new information. Keep your chin up."

Sergeant Dace stood and walked down the stairs to the front door and Beth followed. He turned toward Beth and outstretched his hand.

"Goodbye, Beth, good luck. Call me if you need anything."

"Thank you, Sergeant Dace."

He dropped Beth's hand and she let him out.

Beth walked upstairs and into the kitchen to call Louise.

"I just spoke to our local investigator. He is afraid of my mother trying to get to our kids. He suggested you call your local investigator and have a detail on your kids and on you and Joey."

Louise gasped. "Does he really believe your mother would hurt us?"

"He doesn't put anything past her. He just wants us to be careful and stay safe. Please, call. It'll make me feel better."

"Okay, I'll talk to Joey when he gets home. If Joey agrees, I'll call first thing in the morning."

"Good, I'm glad we finally found people who listen and believe us. The hard part will be proving what my mother did."

"Yeah, that's the hard part."

Chapter 26

Thursday, Beth, Louise and Joey met Laura Nelson at the Five Stars.

"Before I start, here's a contract I need one of you to sign, along with an estimate of my fees."

Beth, Joey, and Louise looked at the estimate.

"Any questions?" Laura asked "Are my fees something you can handle?"

Louise looked at Laura, who was sitting across the table from her. "Joey and I have decided we will pay for the investigation. Yes, this is what we expected." Joey nodded in agreement.

"Good, I started the investigation yesterday. I drove out to Maple Grass and spoke to Detective Rasp. We both agreed that since Johnston is such a close-knit community, they should not be involved in the investigation. We both also agree that unless Delilah is stopped, we fear she will continue in the same manner. Detective Rasp is interested in taking the case. He said once my investigation is complete and my report is written, he will take it to the states attorney's office for possible prosecution."

Beth began to cry. "I'm thankful that law enforcement feels the same way we do. We have been trying to get someone to listen and believe us." Beth sighed through her tears. "What a relief."

Beth signed the contract while Joey wrote out a check and handed it to Laura. Beth handed Laura a copy of all three death certificates, and Louise handed her a list of medications she knew Helen was taking.

"Now that we have a signed contract, I'll go down to the medical examiner's office. I spoke to Rob last night. He said you and your husband are good people. He asked me to give your case extra attention and, of course, I will. You're lucky to have such a good friend."

"I know it. Rob and Cheryl are great."

"Well, any other questions or concerns from any of you?"

Beth asked. "How long can we expect the investigation to last? How will you notify us of what you've found?"

"I should be able to wrap up my initial investigation within a couple of weeks. If you don't mind, I will complete my investigation and provide you with my initial report at the end. That will be quicker for me since I won't have to stop and give you a call every step of the way. If something requires a decision, I will definitely call."

"Sounds good to me." Beth turned toward her uncle and his wife. "What do you think Louise and Joey?"

"Sounds good," Joey said. "I assume you'll call Beth?"

"Yes, since my initial contact was with Beth and since she signed the contract, I will call her. Louise and Joey, feel free to call me if you need to. Is that all right with you, Beth?"

"Absolutely, Louise or Joey can call."

"Okay, then," Laura said as she started to put her papers in her briefcase. "It was a pleasure meeting all of you. If there are no more questions, I'll get to work."

All three responded, "No more questions."

Laura rose from her seat, shook everyone's hand and left. As Laura walked away, Beth and Louise looked at each other and let out a sigh of relief.

א

Later that week Laura interviewed Louise, Joey, and Beth. Two weeks later, Beth received Laura's initial investigative report. It was directed to Detective Rasp. In it she explained that she had visited Chicago's medical examiner's office where she was told, after review of all three death certificates, that none of them were filled out properly. The certificates were missing vital information.

The actual cause of death had not been explained.

The letter went on to explain that Laura met with Doctor Bonnie Kale, a pathologist at the medical examiner's office. Doctor Kale explained that the cause of death on the certificates was nondescript, again verifying that vital information was missing.

Laura had continued the discussion with Doctor Kale about possible causes of death after giving her a quick description of the case background, including a list of medications that Louise believed Helen to be taking. Laura wrote:

> *Doctor Kale said there were several ways that someone could cause death using a combination of the medications Helen presumably was taking, and each combination would cause different side effects. These medications would have shown up in an autopsy. Since neither an autopsy nor blood tests were performed, these drugs could still be found in the organs of the deceased if they were exhumed – even after an extended length of time.*

Laura went on to explain that Doctor Kale consulted with a toxicologist who said the only exception to this would be the sleeping medication known as Halcion, which was one of the medications Louise believed Helen was given. He also indicated that any bruises should have been documented at the time of death.

Laura explained that Doctor Kale seemed concerned with the issues presented. She said they were definitely suspicious, and she would be willing to take a look at the bodies should they be exhumed. The letter ended with Laura asking Beth to call her after reading the report.

Beth put down the report and gave Laura a call.

"Hi Laura, this is Beth, I finished reading your report. It sounds promising."

"Don't get your hopes up too much. We still have a long way to go. I spoke to both Detective Rasp and Doctor Kale yesterday. They are willing to collaborate once we get the bodies exhumed. Unfortunately, I believe the only way to make that happen, at least for Helen and Clara, is to get the Johnston criminal investigator involved. At this point, they have jurisdiction of the bodies."

Beth's body stiffened while listening intently.

Laura continued. "I hate to get them involved, but I think we have to. I also called Water's Funeral Home in Johnston. They handled all three bodies. The records for all three of your family members have mysteriously disappeared. They apologized, and said they had never lost records before. All three were in the same folder with your parents' name on it. The folder just went missing."

"Funny how that happened," Beth answered with disgust.

"Well Beth, I think I have done all I can for now. I'll call the Johnston Police Department and talk to their investigator. He'll probably want a copy of my report. After that, until the bodies are exhumed, there is nothing else for me to do. If something comes up in Johnston that needs my attention, I'll get on it. Otherwise, call me if you decide you need something else."

"Okay, thanks for all you've done. This is the most hope I've had."

"Remember, don't get your hopes up too high."

"I'll remember. Thanks for everything."

Beth pushed down the receiver on her phone, released it and immediately dialed Louise's number. She relayed her conversation with Laura. Beth heard Louise exhale.

"I wish we didn't have to get anyone in Johnston involved. I don't think they'll do anything," Louise said. "I feel the only way anything will happen is to have it investigated in Chicago. They seem to believe your mother is guilty."

"They at least think it seems suspicious. I think they would be able to handle my Grandma Margaret's investigation but not Aunt Clara or Grandma Helen. I agree. I wish we didn't have to get Johnston involved."

"Well, all we can do is follow Laura's advice and see what happens."

"Yeah, unfortunately, it's all we can do."

Beth heard a click on her phone. "There's a call waiting, Louise, I'll call you if I hear anything else."

Beth answered the call. "Hi Beth. This is Laura. I just spoke to Detective Kemp from the Johnston Police

Department. He will be calling you for some additional information. I agree with you, he doesn't seem too eager to investigate. Let me know if you need anything else."

"Thanks, Laura."

Beth once again felt herself against a brick wall. *I finally hoped we were getting somewhere, only to be shot back down. Will anyone ever help me?*

ℵ

Detective Kemp phoned the following morning and scheduled an interview with Beth for the next day.

"It's about an eight hour drive from Johnston to Chicago, so I'll see you around ten a.m. Is that okay?" the detective said.

"Yes, I'll be here."

When Detective Kemp arrived, Beth thought it strange that he asked for a tour of Beth's house.

"You have a large house. It's nicely furnished and really clean," he said. "What does your husband do?"

"He's an engineer."

"Well it seems like he makes a good living. It doesn't appear that you are in any financial trouble."

"No, we're not. What does that have to do with anything?"

"Do your parents have a will?"

"I don't know. Again, what does that matter?" Beth said with some agitation.

"If your parents were imprisoned, who would

handle their estate?"

"I don't know."

"Aren't you an only child?"

"Yes."

"Well then, wouldn't you expect to be responsible for your parents' estate if they were unable to oversee it themselves?"

"I don't know what arrangements my parents may have made. That's their business."

"Wouldn't it become your business?"

"I don't know."

"Well, that's all I need. I'll be leaving now. I'll let you know what my investigation turns up."

Beth was furious. The detective didn't even mention the case or ask any questions about it. She wondered what kind of investigation he would conduct.

א

Three days later Detective Kemp telephoned Beth.

"The coroner that responded to your Aunt Clara's death has resigned. We determined he was diagnosed with dementia last year and kept the diagnosis from us. His report is full of holes; vital information is missing, so we don't really know what happened. I don't know what else we can do."

Beth felt all the energy drain from her body as she slumped into a chair, *She's going to get away with murder,* she thought. *I hope we can exhume the bodies; that's the only way we will be able to get any evidence.*

Beth called Laura Nelson to give her an update.

"Let me see what I can do. Maybe I can get Detective Rasp and Doctor Kale to petition the courts, allowing them to take possession of the bodies. Beth, I'm so sorry."

"Thanks, Laura."

Laura called back a couple hours later.

"The district attorney was willing to file a petition, but when he talked to Detective Kemp, he was told that the Johnston district attorney will file a counter petition. They are unwilling to give up jurisdiction. I think our hands are tied. I'll get my final report written and send you a copy."

"Okay, Laura, thanks," Beth answered with a heavy heart

Beth had cried so much over the last several months, she didn't think she had any tears left, but as she hung up the phone, she fell to the floor and cried uncontrollably.

 я

When Beth brought in the mail the next day, two letters caught her eye: one from Laura Nelson Investigations and one from the Johnston, Wisconsin district attorney's office. Beth opened Laura's letter first. It was her final investigative report. She then opened the letter from Johnston's district attorney. The letter read:

*Although I find these deaths to be highly sus-
picious, I don't have concrete evidence to provide
a basis to disinter the bodies. However, pursuant
to §69.18 (4), Ms. Jasdam could apply to the court
for an order for disinterment and re-interment if she
does not agree. Should she obtain such an order, I
believe that Johnston would have to do the disinterment in order to preserve the chain of custody. Also,
before the bodies would be disinterred, we would
need permission from the executor of the estate,
Mike Marin.*

Beth folded the letter and returned it to the envelope. She was in a state of shock as she thought to
herself, *My father will never get permission to have the
bodies exhumed; my mother would never allow him to.
The only hard evidence they could get is from the bodies they refuse to exhume. I'm defeated.*

Chapter 27

Snow was still falling when Beth and Edward returned home from the hospice memorial service. The moon was shining brightly in the clear sky. It reminded Beth of the night she walked to town with her father and the boys. As they walked towards the house, Edward put his arm around Beth's waist.

"You're shaking and you hardly said a word all the way home. What's wrong?"

"I spent the trip home thinking about my grand-mothers and Aunt Clara." Beth stopped and looked at Edward. "When I walked through the doorway of the community center and noticed Leo sitting next to my mother, my heart sank into my stomach as I wondered if he would be her next victim."

They walked into the house. Beth removed her coat

and boots, walked out to the sun porch and turned on the gas fireplace. She sat at the same loveseat she was at earlier in the day, only now she was watching the snow instead of the birds while completing her thoughts.

She remembered receiving a call after she finished her conversation with Laura Nelson. When she answered, it was Ruth, her cousin Steven's wife.

"Beth, I have some terrible news."

"What is it?"

"Steven is dead."

Beth gasped in shock. "Oh my gosh, Ruth, what happened?"

"He came home yesterday after spending the last two weeks in Johnston."

"Did he spend time with my parents?" Beth interrupted.

"Yes he did. He didn't feel well when he came home. He went to bed last night and never woke up. The coroner said it was heart failure."

Acknowledgment

I would like to offer a special thank you to the members of the Green Bay Writers Guild for their support and inspiration. I would also like to thank everyone who has encouraged me, for the past thirty years, to write Bethany's story. A special thank you to Christine Keleny, whose patience, guidance and incredible editing has allowed this work to become what I always imagined it could be.

About the Author

L.L. Mecazani grew up in the Windy City, then later moved to Wisconsin, where she still resides with her husband and family. *Delilah* is her debut novel. She is a member of the Green Bay Writer's Guild, the Wisconsin Writer's Association and the Mystery Writers of America. Visit her website at: llmecazani.com.

⋊

If you enjoyed this story, please leave a review on your favorite website.

Thank you